So I Went up the Council

– GARRY FROSTICK –

To Mick

Best wishes from

Garry Frostick

Christmas 2013

FASTPRINT PUBLISHING
PETERBOROUGH, ENGLAND

Garry Frostick

www.fast-print.net/store.php

So I Went up the Council
Copyright © Garry Frostick 2011

ISBN 978-184426-954-9

First published 2011 by
FASTPRINT PUBLISHING
Peterborough, England.

An environmentally friendly book printed and bound in England
by www.printondemand-worldwide.com

This book is made entirely of chain-of-custody materials

Garry Frostick

This book is dedicated to the memory of my father.

With grateful thanks to my wife Yvonne for her support and encouragement in its compilation and to Penny Clark for her assistance in its production.

Garry Frostick

Chapter 1

It was another regular Monday morning at Creekleigh District Council. The wind was blowing its icy blast directly off the Irish Sea as the offices opened for their weekly business. The staff of the Housing Department, or more particularly the receptionist, sat waiting expectantly for the early arrival of the regular Monday morning complaints that had been manifesting themselves amongst their tenants since the office had closed its doors at 5 o'clock on Friday night. What will it be today she wondered; drains, refuse collection, maintenance, noisy neighbours? She didn't have to wait long as in walked one of her regulars.

Sidney Saines was a council house tenant in the town and had been since his marriage in 1948. Now widowed he lived in a warden assisted bungalow in relatively close proximity to the Council Offices which, unfortunately for the housing department, made it extremely convenient for him to 'go up the council', as he liked to refer to his necessary visits, to air any grievance he might have.

As he approached her desk the receptionist smiled in recognition. She had known Sidney for a number of years

1

and whilst his complaints were normally trivial, as far as she was concerned, she had learnt that as long as he felt that his perceived problem was being taken seriously then he would be content. There were others of a far less even disposition than Sidney and so, whilst she was not entirely happy to have her working week commence with what she was sure would be a complaint; she was at least content in the knowledge that it was coming from Sid.

'Good morning Mr Saines, weather not too good today is it.'

'No Miss Treacher' replied Sid 'I've had to walk all this way up to your office in this bloody weather because your blokes cant keep a simple appointment.'

Miss Treacher reached under her desk and took out the departmental complaint book. 'Now Mr Saines, what are we supposed to have done this time and haven't't'.

'It's me ballcock or more correctly next doors.'

Ah the old ballcock problem thought Miss T.

'And just what had we promised you Mr Saines?'

'Well' replied Sid, 'last Wednesday I came up here to complain to your mate about the thumping that goes right through my house every time next door flushes his toilet.'

Wednesday was Miss Treacher's day off as she attended the local college of further education for her part time ONC Business Studies Course.

'He comes home from the pub at two in the morning, god knows where he has been since last orders, and when he pulls the chain the knocking of the pipes and whistling of the water is enough to wake the dead.'

'Your mate, I don't know her name but she gets her hair

colour out of a bottle, giggles when she talks to you and has what looks like bloody wind chimes hanging from her ears.'

'Her name's Tracy' interjected the receptionist

'Well, whatever her name is, she said that she would report the matter to your Mr Smith and that someone would contact me before the weekend. I waited in all Friday but no bugger came, only the milkman after his money. Do you know how much a litre of semi-skimmed is now from him? It's a damned sight cheaper in Tesco's I told him and do you know what he told me? Well I couldn't repeat it but I can tell you he ain't getting any Christmas Box from me this year. Anyway, as I said, I waited and no one came and I want to know why.'

'Let me check in the complaints register Mr Saines, I am sure there is a good reason why you weren't visited if we promised to call.'

Miss Treacher was well versed in dealing with the local complaints of the town's council tenants and even adroit in covering for the shortcomings of the council's limited professional staff. If something had not been done she often found herself having to explain that it was because of a more urgent life-threatening event that had diverted the relevant officer's attention. However, there were also times when her sympathies were with the tenant who she believed wanted her to say that 'I know we are all bastards and that our sole purpose for being here is to serve your every need!

However on this occasion Miss T was able to advise Sidney that at 15:35, on Thursday of last week the council's maintenance officer has been advised of the offending problem. But that as the source of the offending disturbance was not in Sid's house, but in that of the adjoining terrace, the operative had been asked to call at that address.

'What bloody use is that' exclaimed Sid. 'If he called during opening times he wouldn't have found the bugger in, he would have needed to go up to The White Horse. That's why I said he should visit me.'

'But' explained Miss Treacher, 'how could a call at your house resolve the problem of your neighbours plumbing?'

For a moment Sid was lost for a reply, an unusual situation, but continued to justify his claim that he should have been visited, as it was he who made the complaint. It was then that the receptionist noticed in the complaint register that Sid's neighbour, a Mr Walter Baxter, had indeed received a visit from the Council on Friday at 9:10 and had, according to the report, 'rectified the fault in the main cold water feeder tank'.

On being told this Sidney was also politely asked if he had been disturbed by the noise of his neighbours plumbing since Friday morning. He thought for a moment and then confirmed he hadn't heard it but just assumed that his neighbour had been too pissed to come home over the weekend and so hadn't used the toilet.

Sid remained unhappy that he hadn't been contacted and told that the problem had been rectified but grudgingly thanked Miss Treacher for her help and that he hoped her mother's legs were better.

Sid had been at school with the receptionist's mother Ethel and, as in any small town, he was aware of many of the afflictions affecting his contemporaries and in the case of Ethel it was her legs

As Sid walked out of the council offices into the morning

rain that had eased to a drizzle Miss Treacher turned to the next damp customer, or client as she was now advised to call members of the public, standing at her desk.

'It's about the dog mess on the estate.'

She reached for her ever-expanding loose-leaf register.

As he reached his front door Sid noticed that his garden, which was his pride and joy, was in need of a clear up as the weekend had brought its regular collection of chip papers, sweet wrappers, beer cans, bottles and other paraphernalia associated with a grassed area located approximately 15 minutes staggering time from a town centre to a local council housing estate. 'Bloody kids, bloody drunks' muttered Sid as he went inside and returned with a black sack. If this tight fisted council spent more money on rubbish bins and less on fancy offices it might help this litter problem.

Whilst the cleaning up was by now a regular feature of Monday mornings Sid was continually amazed at the distance the material had travelled to get to his front garden. There were fish and chips wrappers from the 'Happy Plaice' which Sid estimated was over half an hour away on foot, and tin foil containers that he took as being from the new Chinese take-away that had recently moved into the old 'Fisherman's Rest Restaurant' near the river quay. Sid had also noted how, over the years, the nature of the litter had changed. When he had first moved into the bungalow, thirteen years ago, at the end of the nineteen eighties he was sure that there were more soft drink than beer cans and that he never found anything relating to sexual matters. But now it was not uncommon to find used contraceptives draped on his front fence as if placed there as trophies of an evening's achievements. Even the confectionary wrappers had changed from Mars bars and milk chocolate to plastic mint packets and muesli bars.

Sid went back into his bungalow clutching his plastic bag and took it through the house into the rear garden and placed its contents into the dustbin muttering to himself that he expected the bin men to spill half of it back onto his garden when they collected it on Wednesday.

Bloody contract collectors, he thought, only interested in emptying as many bins as they can in the shortest possible time. No sense of civic pride and service that the old Council's bin men used to have.

Sid prided himself on being a retired manual worker who could identify with the old council's refuse collectors. In the old days, if you wanted to get rid of a mattress or something bulky, you could always give one of them a couple of bob and it would be disposed of. Nowadays it's all too much effort and if it can't fit into one or two regulation black sacks then it won't be collected without an exorbitant charge. Sid also could not see the advantage of recycling which Creekleigh Council had been trying to encourage its local residents to embrace. He believed that the publicity in the form of advertising, posters, leaflets and mail shots had generated more paper than the recycling programme would collect, or it was just a ploy to enhance the amount of paper circulating in the area and so help to justify the project!

In its recycling drive the council had also initiated cans, plastics and glass collection points in the towns two main car parks but as Sid only possessed an aged bike he had no intention of separating all his limited recyclable waste and then doing what he considered was the council's job of taking his tins and bottles to a disposal point. That's why he paid his poll tax, council tax or whatever it was called nowadays.

Chapter 2

S id had had a relatively poor childhood having been one of 4 children, 2 brothers and a stepsister. His father had been a general labourer and occasional chimney sweep with his mother taking in washing and serving in the local pub (Crown and Anchor) in the evenings. His father had fought in the First World War before Sid was born having served in Palestine with the camel corps. He had volunteered as soon as war was declared, albeit he was under age, and after initial training he had been sent overseas to what was then Palestine to see active service with a number of fellow local recruits. Had his father waited to be called up he would almost certainly have found himself posted to France or Belgium and had to fight in the trenches. Instead on his eighteenth birthday he found himself far from home in Egypt in charge of a small group of camels at the foot of the Great Pyramid. From that period on he had a hatred of camels and declared that they smelt foul at both ends of their body and had a temper to match.

This information he had imparted to Sid who throughout his life could not see or hear reference to a camel without thinking of his father.

Despite his hard life Sid's father, also called Sidney to add to the confusion in later life of correspondence both personal and official, lived to the grand old age of 92. Whilst only 5ft 3 inches in height he had been quite a muscular individual with a quick fiery temper and a passion for women and Woodbines, but not necessarily in that order.

However, despite this predilection for the females and his very much chauvinistic attitude Sid recalled that his father had always shown strong affection for his mother and his brothers and sister and that whilst during the depression of the 1920s they had suffered considerable hardship he had always tried to provide for the family by doing whatever work, however menial, was available to ensure that some income came to the family.

For her part his mother Elizabeth always made sure that her children were clean and whilst there was little money for new clothes or shoes she ensured that what they had was washed and darned.

It was with this background of the need to make every penny count that Sid still approached life not spending unless he had to and when he did he made sure he got value for money and god help the trader or supplier that either overcharged him or sold him poor quality goods.

Sid's mother had been taller than his father, pretty he remembered, with sharp features and her dark hair tied in a tight bun.

His older sister Emily normally had the responsibility for putting him to bed in the evenings as his mother would have been working in the local pub. It was probably because of this fact that of the three siblings it was his sister that he still felt the greatest affinity with and affection for.

In fact he had not spoken to his younger brother Stan since the death of his mother almost 30 years ago when there had been an argument about money.

Sid's bungalow consisted of a small sitting room with an original fireplace that had been blocked in and replaced with a gas fire that attempted to give the effect of a burning flame but only succeeded in looking like a gas fire pretending to be what it wasn't.

There was no central heating and therefore his only means of heating his water for washing up, baths etc., was by an electric emersion heater. Therefore, bath night was restricted to one day a week, Sundays, when Sid would combine the heating of the water for both his hot tub and clothes washing.

The walls of his lounge were covered in magnolia painted chip wood wallpaper. Pictures and paintings, none of which had cost any more than a few pence, had been acquired from numerous sources including his daughter-in-law, who was a prolific amateur artist, and also from the local charity shops.

The lounge was simply furnished with a two-seater settee Sid had purchased from the Co-op furniture store about 20 years ago and a battered armchair he had recently had reupholstered. There was also a small coffee table that had originally been the middle-sized part of a nest of three, and a long narrow sideboard that sat below his lounge window. This window overlooked the road outside his house from which he kept a watching brief on all movements in the street.

Numerous family photographs adorned the top of this piece of furniture including pictures of his late wife, children and grandchildren.

The room was dominated by a large dresser that housed Sid's collection of commemorative mugs dating back to the reign of Queen Victoria. Tucked into the tops of these were numerous receipts, bills and various other pieces of paper containing long forgotten notes of out dated pieces of information.

A large Decca television stood in the corner of the room on top of which was a small portable CD player.

Hanging from the ceiling, which was a nicotine cream colour, was a single pendant lampshade and a 60 watt bulb which, on a dark winters, evening gave the room an eerie glow as the light from the low wattage tried to penetrate the deep orange colour of the shade and its accompanying tassels.

Access to his lounge was secured through a small entrance hallway that contained a coat stand, a small table and a house brick that he used to prop his front door open when he went on his regular patrol of the front garden to clear the litter and debris that generally found its way over his privet hedge and onto his lawn. The brick had been frequently employed ever since he had ventured out late one evening to remove some polystyrene containers he had spotted and had been locked out of his house by a sudden gust of wind blowing his door closed behind him. He had then spent a great deal of time and effort getting back into the house via the kitchen window which had fortunately been left open given the warmth of the summer evening.

Leading from the small hallway was a doorway into Sid's bathroom, which was painted in a bright pink with white tiles around the bath and basin. On the floor was brown linoleum with a mock floorboard pattern. This was overlain on floorboards of a higher quality and greater durability than the cheap flooring used to cover it. Behind the toilet cistern, on the windowsill, was a knitted Spanish doll in a flamenco skirt under which was a spare toilet roll.

Sid's bedroom led directly off the lounge. Despite the small size of the room Sid insisted on sleeping in a double bed and therefore with a chest of drawers and a large wardrobe also within the room, there was very little space for circulation. As in the lounge, the top of the chest of drawers was festooned with family photographs. Within the drawers below were numerous unopened polythene bags containing unworn clothes including vests, underpants, socks and shirts. These had been acquired as presents or purchased in sales as bargains but then never used as there was always some life left in his regular clothing. This resistance to using new clothes was a throwback to his childhood days when he never had the luxury of a choice of clothing.

Sid's kitchen, like the rest of the property, was in Estate Agents terms 'compact' and functional. In his view it was too small to swing a cat. However, within the confined space Sid was able to fit a small kitchen table alongside his sink unit, refrigerator and gas cooker. A portable radio, permanently tuned to the local BBC radio station, sat on the work surface alongside a basic microwave oven. His kitchen cupboards contained vast numbers of canned foods, which he stockpiled just in case he became housebound for any length of time, and had to rely on a store cupboard to see him through any confinement. On a recent visit his son, having need to retrieve an item from the depository, had been amazed at the size and nature of the tinned food he had unearthed and had wondered how long his father would have had to be incarcerated to get through what he estimated was over two dozen tins of baked beans, a case of sardines, catering packs of tinned new potatoes, in excess of a dozen cans of Ye Olde Oak Ham and 10 tins of Californian prunes in syrup. Combined with the numerous tins of soup of various flavours and hundreds of tea bags his son considered that his father had enough provisions to withstand a siege let alone a short period of incapacity.

From the kitchen there was a back door that led into Sid's rear garden.

The garden was only eight metres long and marginally wider than the width of the house. His garden, and in particular the greenhouse, was his pride and joy and even on a winter's day it looked neat and well managed. A bird table sat at one corner of the garden whilst in the other was a shed that contained all of Sid's tools, garden implements and his trusty, and now a bit rusty, Raleigh cycle

Chapter 3

During his self imposed Friday at home waiting for the council to call about next doors plumbing, Sid had been studying work which had been going on at the council offices which he could clearly see, if he stood on his front door step and leaned at a precarious angle to his left. Throughout the day a structure had been gradually rising into the air from the corner of the council employees' car park that appeared to Sid to be a "bloody great aerial."

He had taken the opportunity that morning on his visit to the council offices to inspect it close up and confirmed to his own satisfaction that it was an aerial but far grander than that which sat on his roof and provided a roosting point for all the incontinent pigeons in the town.

Sid also began to consider the point that it was since Friday that his BBC2 reception had become severely impaired with a "wire netting type effect" helping to distort the picture. With this thought in mind Sid went into his small back garden and looked up at his aerial and then into the near distance towards the council's offices. Just as I thought, he said to himself, my aerial is directly in line, they must be blocking my BBC2 signal. I'll see about this. So after a quickly taken lunch of savaloy and chips Sid strode off to the council offices for the second time that day. He stood for a while in the car park first looking up at the aerial and then back towards his house and was by now convinced that his hypothesis was correct insofar as the council were interfering with his television reception (albeit only BBC2 which he very rarely watched except for nature programmes).

Sid's next problem was who to complain to at the council as he stood there looking at the notice board displaying the list of departments and their various functions.

Planning - piss poor planning in respect of location thought Sid but probably not them. Highways- no, Treasurers- no, Chief Executives - what the hell do they do thought Sid, but no. Parks and Recreation- no, then his eyes alighted on the familiar Housing Department. Well thought Sid, the aerial is interfering with my aerial that is fixed to one of their houses so they should at least be concerned about it.

Miss Treacher had just returned from her subsidised canteen lunch when she saw the familiar figure of Sid Saines enter through the swing doors of the office. He was, she estimated from the age of her mother, into his late '70s. He was a tallish man of about 6ft, always clean shaven but his dark complexion gave him a swarthy almost gypsy like appearance consistent with a man who had spent his life as a labourer and mostly in outdoor employment.

'Good afternoon Mr Saines, unusual to see you twice in one day, how can we help you this time?'

Sid then explained in words of mostly one syllable the impact that the council's new structure in their car park was having on his television's reception and wanted to know what the mast in their car park was for and what they were going to do about it. This was a new complaint for the receptionist and one, which she was pretty sure, was not her province to deal with.

'I can understand your anger and concern if there is something we at the council have done to affect your enjoyment of watching television but I am sure it's not the fault or responsibility of the Housing Department.'

'Well who is to blame then' asked Sid.

'I don't honestly know' replied the perplexed Miss Treacher, 'but I will try to find out.'

With that she began to ring round to her colleagues on the reception desks of the other departments. Eventually she put down the receiver and told Sidney that it was the Water Authority.

'Water Authority be buggered' said Sid 'It's in your car park; you can't pass the blame onto them. Foul tasting water, holes dug in the road and not being backfilled for weeks, sky high water rates maybe but not that sodding aerial.'

'Well I am afraid it is the Water Authority Mr Saines. As you know, our offices are on a hill.'

'Don't I know it; I believe you built it on one on purpose to deter the likes of me from visiting.'

Miss Treacher smiled to herself and thought if only. She continued

'The Water Authority have erected the aerial as part of their electronic telemetry monitoring service for flood warnings in this part of the county.'

'Oh' said Sid not fully or even half understanding what

she had said. 'So you mean to say that it has nothing to do with you then.'

'No, only that we provided the land onto which the structure has been built but that is purely a contractual arrangement with our Chief Executive's Department'.

So that's what they do, thought Sid.

'Well who do I complain to then?'

Miss Treacher reached for her complaints register, which at the front had an index of those other bodies to whom she could 'pass the buck' in the event of a misdirected complaint.

'Now let me see' she said 'I have a contact number here for the general headquarters in Preston'.

'Where!' exclaimed Sid, 'that's no bloody good to me, haven't they got a local office.'

'Not with any inquiry section with public access' she confirmed.

Sid thought for a moment and then exclaimed that as it was a television in a council house that was experiencing the problem it was the landlord's duty to rectify the situation and so what were the housing department going to do about it?

Miss T sighed and opened her complaints book and began to write. She explained that the matter would be looked into and that he would receive a formal reply from the council just as soon as the situation could be investigated.

Sid thanked her and said that 'He anticipated a letter in the next seven days or else and that they wouldn't like else'.

As he left, Sid had a thought and suggested to the despairing receptionist that maybe they could reposition the aerial so that it didn't align with his and offered his directional services to the council if that would assist. Pleased that he had left the offices on what he thought was a helpful and positive note Sid headed back to his bungalow.

Chapter 4

It was Thursday morning. Sid was awakened by his telephone ringing. Nobody ever telephoned him at that time of day and normally his only calls were from his son or daughter, or double glazing salesmen, but that's another story. Gingerly, Sid picked up the receiver, it was his sister-in-law.

'Sid that is you isn't it, are you all right, we thought you might be dead.'

Sid was momentarily lost for words but then responded 'of course I'm not dead I'm talking to you ain't I.'

'I know' replied Barbara 'But I have just been reading today's local paper and you're in it under the obituaries.'

Again there was a moments quiet and then she continued, 'I didn't think it was true but as it is in the paper.'

If she had only thought a bit more, he mused; she would have known that the paper, as usual, had cocked something up again. He recalled when he had won the best- kept front garden competition that it had referred to him as Mr Stains.

After a few more exchanges of conversation about each other's general health Barbara rang off with a promise that she and her husband would pop round some time and visit him.

A little confused, Sid went to the front door and returned with the weekly edition of The Creekleigh Gazette. Hurriedly he turned to the births, deaths and marriages section and scanned the columns. Sure enough under the "In Memoriam" column was the insertion.

"Sidney Saines (74) passed away on 27th February at a nursing home after a short illness. Family and friends will sadly miss him".

Bugger, thought Sidney, it seems like someone does think I'm dead and only 74. Soon the telephone in his small bungalow began to ring with people calling just to see if it was true that he was dead. He was deeply touched by their concern but puzzled that they should be telephoning him to see if he was alive or not.

As the calls began to subside Sid decided that a dead man should at least eat and made himself some breakfast and strong black Camp Coffee. He then began to muse about the obituary and its origins and eventually concluded that it must have been a distant relative that had been living in one of the local villages. Happy in his analysis Sid put on his cap and coat and went for a walk into the town to collect his pension and to buy a loaf of bread and some frozen peas.

As he walked up the familiar High Street he had known for almost the whole of his 78 years of life he felt strange. People he hardly ever spoke to or was only on nodding acquaintanceship, came up to him and said how pleased they were that he wasn't dead. Others just stopped in their tracks and stared and then broke into smiles. One old female acquaintance came up to him and touched him and said 'Oh you are real Sid'.

By this time the novelty was beginning to wear off and Sid found himself barking back at her saying 'That of course he was bloody real and that he wasn't a sodding ghost.'

As he entered Iceland Sid was greeted warmly by the staff who had been saddened that morning that they may have lost one of their regular and more colourful customers. That was until Sid turned the corner by the frozen vegetable section and found himself face to face with Mrs Ethel Treacher. On seeing what she thought was an apparition her legs buckled beneath her and she had to be helped from the diced carrots and sliced green beans that she had toppled towards in her distress.

'Goodness, you gave me a fright Sid' she said as she gathered her senses and pair of walking sticks together. '

'Me and Helen had read about what we thought was you in the paper this morning and she had said she hadn't seen you at the council since Monday.'

Once Sid's concern for Ethel's welfare had been satisfied through the kindly staff making her a cup of tea and sitting her down on a stool next to the cut bread display, he tried to explain to her who it actually was in the newspaper. However as she explained 'As far as the local town residents were concerned there was only one Sid Saines.'

Amen to that thought Helen.

Friday arrived and the number of phone calls had reduced dramatically as had the doorstep callers to his bungalow and the shock that Sid had also personally experienced. So it was that that evening Sid settled down to watch television. As he flicked aimlessly with his remote control he happened onto BBC2 between programmes and as he waited to see what was on next he was advised by an announcement, over a background picture of the largest aerial he had ever seen, that the BBC apologised to viewers in the West of England who had been experiencing poor quality reception for the last 7 days. This had been caused by the need to carry out emergency maintenance work on the local transmitter.

Sid sat silently for a moment and thought to himself I am sure that the picture quality used to be better than this before that aerial on the council car park was erected.

Chapter 5

Later that night Sid was just settling down for bed, he had removed his teeth and slippers when he heard the most almighty crash, or so he thought, outside his bungalow. He hurried to the window expecting to see a car or two in some sort of collision as he always contended the road outside his home was like a racetrack, albeit the geometry of the road prevented vehicles from travelling above 30mph. However, there was no sign of any carnage in the road but what Sid did hear was some of the ripest language he had heard in years coming from a woman, he guessed at being in her early forties, banging on the front door of his neighbours house with what appeared to be half a house brick in her hand.

'Come on out I know you're in there you dirty bastard' she screamed. This torrent of abuse continued with a small gathering crowd of onlookers standing on their front steps or looking around their curtains as Sid was doing.

'How dare you try to mess around with my daughter you dirty old ★★★★★★'

As the expletives got louder and more frequent so the narrative of what Sid's neighbour had allegedly done became lost in the torrent of abuse. At this point the brick that the woman had been using to thud against the front door was sent crashing through the bay window whilst in the distance Sid could hear the wail of the approaching local constabulary vehicle. As the police arrived the woman was still ranting about what the occupant was supposed to have done to her daughter but then the onlookers were stunned as she delivered the sentence

'I know what you have done in the past with little boys you dirty bastard'

A visible change ran around the assembled group of onlookers who, until that point, had been mildly amused at the antics of the woman and her sounding off at the alleged misdemeanours of Sid's neighbour, who appeared to be either lying very low or, more likely, out.

Bugger me; thought Sid, he must be a child molester, one of them paedophiles I've been reading about in the Mirror.

By this time the local constabulary had arrived outside No.11. The woman PC from the squad car, who Sid thought looked like a female bouncer from the local nightclub with her cropped hair and the way her ample frame placed a considerable strain on her uniform, approached the still screaming banshee in an effort to quieten her rantings. Meanwhile, her male colleague, in the archetypical police manner, addressed the local residents by saying there was nothing to see and that they should all go home.

Gradually they duly obliged and within ten minutes there were only a couple of drunks and a child on a scooter, who Sid thought should have been in bed hours ago, on the pavement outside the house. Sid, however, continued to observe from behind his twitching curtain as the police, like the woman, failed to gain the attention of the occupier. It emerged later that Walter Baxter had seen the approach of the woman and made a hasty retreat over his rear fence and into the communal alleyway behind the property.

As Sid continued to watch the proceedings, with his house lights off so as not to highlight his obvious interest, he noticed that the WPC was opening his front gate and walking up the garden path carefully stepping over the flotsam and jetsam that had begun its regular nightly accumulation in his garden.

Sid opened the door tentatively,

'Yes' he said 'What do you want?'

WPC Charnley was, Sid estimated, no more than 20 years old. Hardly old enough (but certainly big enough) to drive he thought let alone to have the responsibility of police duty.

He was also rather a chauvinist at heart and believed a woman's place was in the home or, at best, should have no higher aspiration than that of a secretary or receptionist. Which was one of the many reasons why he harboured such an overwhelming dislike of Margaret Thatcher.

WPS Charnley explained that she was investigating a disturbance at the house next door and wondered if Sid could be of any assistance.

'Do you have any form of identification' asked Sid although it was blatantly obvious from the activity outside his window and the parked squad car that the WPC was the genuine article. The officer however duly obliged and produced her warrant card. Sid studied it carefully. It looked genuine enough but to be honest if she had shown him her Weight Watchers card Sid would not have known the difference. He simply knew from watching Shaw Taylor on TV that it was the sort of thing that he should ask for before admitting police to his home.

Sid confirmed he had been disturbed by the goings on next door but had not taken very much notice. When asked about his neighbour and if he knew his likely whereabouts he replied that he was not surprised he wasn't in as, in his words, he was a bit of a piss artist and that as it was late on a Friday evening he would probably be in the pub. Most likely The White Horse.

WPC Charnley thanked him, closed her notebook and turned to leave, but as Sid opened the front door she turned to him and asked 'Why haven't you got a chain on your door Mr Saines.'

'Too expensive' responded Sid.

'I am sure if you approached the council they would be willing to supply one either free or for a minimal charge' she said as she again tried to leave.

'Hey, before you go' said Sid 'Can I ask you a question?'

'Certainly'

'Well, that woman who was banging on Walter's front door said something about him interfering with little boys. Is that true?'

'I don't know Mr Saines, all I know is that we were called to deal with a domestic disturbance and we will be carrying out further investigations into the matter. Good night and thank you for your assistance.'

Sid closed the front door and made his way back to his bedroom. As he laid there that night with his alarm clock ticking and the town clock striking the quarter hours he found himself unable to sleep for the thought of what, or who, might be lying in a bed no more than a few feet away on the other side of what he considered were paper-thin walls.

The next morning, after a fitful night's sleep Sid awoke and made himself some breakfast and mused about the previous evening's happenings. As Saturday was market day in the town the road outside Sid's house was generally busy, being one of the main feeder roads into the town centre and therefore for a while Sid was not attracted to anything happening outside his bungalow. This was a rare occurrence as usually very little escaped Sid's attention. However, as he passed the window he noticed that there were a number of people gathered outside his house and, in particular that of his neighbour. Some of them held placards proclaiming 'PAEDOPHILES OUT' and 'SOD OFF'.

Sid gingerly opened his front door.

'Did you know Sid that this bloke next door to you was a bloody child molester' asked a small man in tracksuit bottoms and a very ancient T-shirt supporting the logo 'Keep the GLC'.

'Of course I bloody didn't Arthur' replied Sid 'I just thought he liked a drop of drink'

'Do you know if he's in there asked Arthur' .The size of his beer gut being exaggerated, if that was possible, through the tight fitting T-shirt.

'Don't think so. He certainly wasn't in when the police called last night and I don't recall hearing him come home last night which I normally do'

Once again the police duly arrived in the street.

They are never bloody here when the drunks are throwing their rubbish into my garden thought Sid. The police proceeded to usher the protesters away and again approached the house that was the centre of attraction. Further knocking on the front door and a visit around to the rear of the premises again drew a blank. The police remained for a further 20 minutes until they were content that they had seen off the main body of protesters and then they drove off towards the town centre. Sid remained on the front step talking to Arthur about the previous night and that morning's proceedings.

Arthur, it was revealed, happened to know the woman who had been at the centre of the night's antics and told Sid that apparently her daughter was a barmaid in The White Horse and had been propositioned by Walter.

Arthur did not know the full story but understood it related to her allegedly borrowing some money and him suggesting she could come back to his place to 'pay if off'. But Arthur could not answer the question about the paedophile angle.

Later that morning Sid was sitting in his armchair smoking his pipe of Clan tobacco with the battery removed from his smoke detector, pondering what he should have for lunch when he heard sounds in the bungalow next door. Looking out of his window he was just in time to see Pedro's, the local taxi company's only vehicle, driving away. The buggers come home thought Sidney.

It was at about 2 pm that Sidney heard raised voices coming through the walls of the adjoining bungalow as he was standing at his kitchen sink washing up his single plate and the "Head Gardener" mug his daughter had bought for him from a visit to Wisley. Slowly tugging back the curtain of his front window Sid saw a police squad car and another smaller unmarked car that Sid thought was probably a CID vehicle, as to his mind it was the sort of car he saw detectives in The Bill driving around in.

Sid kept his eye on the road outside his front window, which was nothing unusual, until he saw there was some activity next door with the banging of car doors. He was therefore surprised to see that it wasn't a burly male police officer getting into the second car but two women one of whom he recognised as Miss Anne Johnston who was the District Councils Chief Housing Officer. She was a woman with whom he had crossed swords with in the past when Miss Treacher had been unable to satisfy him.

Well, thought Sid, the plot thickens. What the hell is she doing here on a Saturday afternoon? Normally it's hard enough to get her to do anything during a regular weekday.

The two cars drove away and Sid returned to his washing up. As he stood looking out of his kitchen window into his small back garden Sid could see the familiar and not inconsiderable frame of Walter Baxter walking up and down his garden path drawing heavily on a cigarette.

Being unable to contain his curiosity, which was also by now tinged with apprehension, Sid opened his back door and stepped out into what was a relatively mild winter's day.

'Morning Walter' shouted Sid, who looked up at the sound of a familiar voice.

'Oh hello Sid, didn't see you there.'

The two of them had only been neighbours for about 3 months with Walter having moved into his bungalow following its vacation by old Mrs Jarvis who had died following a heavy fall the day after her 92nd birthday. She had lain on her kitchen floor for 24 hours before she was found. It had been Sid who alerted the housing warden of the lack of activity in the adjoining property, a matter that was still under investigation by the Housing Department.

Despite being neighbours there had been very little interpersonal contact between Sid and Walt. Walter had drawn the opinion that Sid was a nosey individual and didn't want him knowing more about him than he had to and for his part Sid considered Walter to be uncouth and a drunkard and not the sort of person he wanted to be well acquainted with. The result of all this was that they remained on a nodding relationship, acknowledging each others existence and, maybe, exchanging the odd conversation in relation to the weather or what had been thrown into their garden over the weekend.

It was Walter who this time started the conversation.

'I'm off Sid' he said.

'What do you mean off?'

'Just as I said, I'm leaving this afternoon. Taxis coming for me at 4:30 and the Council are arranging to sort out my belongings and have them packed and transported.'

'Bit bloody sudden isn't it'.

'Well you probably saw the situation outside here the other night and again this morning', knowing full well that Sid never missed anything that happened in the road. 'I'm scared and can't get away from this bloody place quick enough. Like a bloody lynch mob they were. That Miss Johnson from the Council Housing Department was here earlier, along with the police, and so between them they have agreed that in everyone's interests that I should leave as soon as practicable, so I'm going today.'

'But where are you going' asked Sid innocently.

'Can't tell you Sid, best you don't know.'

'Back to where you came from' further inquired Sid not to be put off the scent.

'Maybe, maybe.'

Trouble was Sid had never got friendly enough with Walt to find where he had come from in the first place. So realising he wasn't going to have any joy on this matter Sid tried a different tack. Keeping well clear of the paedophile angle, Sid asked if they did any damage to the house the other evening.

'Only broke my bloody window and scattered glass all over me carpet. Bloody woman should keep her nose out of my affairs.'

Sid stayed quiet and let Walter rant on.

'Claims I tried to seduce her daughter. She's a bloody barmaid not a sodding nun, she has a mind of her own and she doesn't need to go bleating home to her mum every time a man makes a pass at her. She'll never make it as a bar maid in this town if she does.'

At this point Walter suddenly turned on his heels and said 'Nice to have known you Sid, look after yourself' and walked back into his kitchen.

This was the last time Sid spoke to his neighbour but he was destined to find out a lot more in the future from an unlikely source.

At 4:30 on the dot Pedro's taxi pulled up outside and Walter Baxter with two large suitcases and a holdall struggled up his garden path, got into the taxi and sped away. To Sid's chagrin he knew not where.

Chapter 6

Sunday morning and Sidney turned on his radio to listen to the Sunday Service. Not because of any strong religious convictions, as these had long been lost, but because the hymns were familiar to him. He thought they all had tunes which was more than could be said for the bloody boom, boom rubbish that he claimed was normally heard coming out of radios these days. Sid had little time for what he classed as modern music, that was anything post Glenn Miller, but nor could he enjoy classical music that he considered was either like cats screeching or had big women wailing in a foreign language. He did, however, have a liking for Don Estelle who he thought had a bloody good voice for such a little bloke.

As it was Sunday morning Sid knew that the warden of his group of sheltered accommodation bungalows would soon be making her regular visit, (one hour later than her normal weekday time). Why this change in schedule Sid had been unable to fathom but assumed it was probably for domestic matters.

At 10:15 Sid's doorbell rang and on the doorstep was the familiar figure of Rita (Sid didn't know her surname). She politely asked Sid if he was okay and hoped that he hadn't been disturbed by the weekend's comings and goings. Rita was in her early thirties, Sid estimated, very thin, painfully so he thought and that a good feed would do her good. She was always in trousers and a close fitting tee shirt, which only served to exaggerate her slender frame. Sid was not aware that she prided herself on her slender appearance and that her late appearance on a Sunday was due to her regular aerobics session at the local gym.

'I'm okay' replied Sid, then, seizing what he thought might be the opportunity to satisfy his curiosity he asked did she know anything about old Baxter's past. If she did know anything she was not willing to impart it to Sid as she admitted that she had been as much in the dark about the situation as she assumed he was. He was just another resident on whom she would look in on once a day and try to help when asked.

Help, thought Sid, bloody good helper she is. He remembered recently that he had had trouble filling in a form for his insurance company following an accident that he had had with his steam iron that had resulted in a severely burnt shirt. At that time he had asked Rita how he should best fill in a part of the form relating to the tenure of his house and another question on 'operational experience' whatever that was. She had told him she was too busy and that besides it was outside of her job description and that he would be better getting one of his children to help or call in at the local Citizens Advice Bureau.

'Well I thought you might have known something about old Baxter, Rita, given your position of authority.'

'I'm only an employee of the council, I am told very little

about the occupants of the bungalows and certainly not their history, apart from medical conditions on a need to know basis.'

'All I know about you Sid is that you transferred from the maisonette opposite after your wife died about 10 years ago.'

Sid could see that he wasn't getting anywhere with stone wall Rita and so he bade her a brisk goodbye and closed his front door.

The front door had hardly closed and Sid was about to settle down in his favourite armchair when the front door bell rang again. What's she forgot to do or tell me now thought Sid who on opening the door was surprised to see Ethel Treacher standing on his doorstep?

'Hello Sid' she said 'I just happened to be passing and thought I must apologise to Sid after my display in Iceland last week'.

'That's okay' responded Sid still surprised to see her. 'Come on in I'll put the kettle on.'

Ethel shuffled into Sid's small living room.

'Take a seat' he shouted from the kitchen, always the gentleman.

As he made the tea Sid thought to himself she was never just passing not with her legs there's more to this visit than to say sorry for last week and what was there to say sorry for anyway. She was clearly overcome with emotion and that's the end of it. Sid returned to the lounge with two teas in mugs, he didn't' have any cups and saucers or at least any that matched.

'Sorry about the mugs, I got that one with an Easter egg

in it from my grandson last year.'

The mug he had passed to Ethel had a picture of a large articulated truck on it with the words 'Yorkie' written in bold red lettering.

'It's very nice.'

'Sugar?' asked Sid passing her an individual white sachet with the logo "Burger King" emblazoned on it.

'No thanks Sid, I always carry a Sweetex with me.'

They sat for a moment sipping tea with Ethel looking round Sid's sitting room.

'Nice pictures Sid' she remarked looking over his shoulder to the far wall on which were hung two watercolours of a cottage by a lake and a seascape.

'Yeah, my daughter-in-law painted them. Lovely colours aren't they. The one with the lake and hills, I believe, is somewhere in the Lake District, the one with the ocean could be anywhere at sea.'

As her eyes left the pictures on the wall she focused on Sid and said quietly 'I have to confess Sid that I have another reason for coming round this morning.'

I thought so mused Sid.

'It's about your old neighbour.'

'What Walt Baxter?'

'Yes. Well you know when he went missing for a day or so recently and the police were looking for him, well he was at my house.'

'What!' exclaimed Sid, who had suddenly become even more interested in his old friend's visit.

'You see he's my step brother.'

Sid's mind began to race. He had known Ethel virtually all his life but had never known that she had a step brother, although he did know that her mother had left her and her father when she was about 12 and that it had been the talk of the school playground and the town. But what he wasn't aware of was that her mother had gone to live up north with another man and that they had had a son, one Walter Baxter.

Ethel then explained to Sid that she had known of Walter's existence for a number of years but it wasn't until about 3 months ago, when he came to live in the town, that she actually met him. It was at that time she had found out that he had spent some time in prison for sexual offences against children and that he was on medication, which was supposed to help his' illness' as she liked to call it.

Sid sat in his armchair spellbound. So it was true what the woman had shouted that evening.

'I felt that I had to come and tell you Sid for two reasons. One I thought I owed it to you as an old friend and ex neighbour of Walters and, secondly, I am so afraid and embarrassed that some people in the town will put two and two together and connect me with him. I couldn't stand the shame and public ridicule.' She began to sob.

Sid didn't know how to react to this. He was not used to dealing with intimate situations and particularly with women. Unable to find any tissues to hand Sid passed Ethel a roll of pastel blue Andrex.

'It's a new one' he said, 'never used'.

She smiled, thanked Sid and blew her nose on a few sheets and handed the roll back to Sid.

'I'm sorry to suddenly burden you with this but we've known each other for so long that I thought I could trust you and I just had to confide in someone.'

Sid felt strangely proud but also aware of the responsibility that Ethel had now placed in his hands. A few hours ago he had been avid in his quest for details of Walter Baxter's past and possible future, but now he felt he knew almost too much but not enough to stop him asking 'Do you know where he is now?'

'All I know Sid is that he has been moved to another district where he will be re-housed but with more strict medical supervision. It was the mixture of medication and alcohol that led to his latest problem with the barmaid and hence the fracas that ensued the other night with her mother coming round the house. How she knew of his past history I don't know but I believe it may be an unlucky coincidence that she and her daughter had also only recently arrived in the town from the north and somehow must have been aware of his earlier wrong doings. I understand that when he did what he did a few years ago, all of the papers up there were full of the story.' She began to sob again but this time Sid was ready with the Andrex.

Sid was about to make further enquiries of Walter's past when a car pulled up outside Sid's house that he did not recognise but he did know the driver as she got out. It was Ethel's daughter from the Council.

'Sid' said Ethel.' Promise me that our conversation will remain a secret between you and me, Helen doesn't know the truth and I would die if she did.'

'Sure' replied Sid feeling he couldn't say anything else while feeling strangely privileged to know something the majority of the town folk would have loved to know.

The doorbell rang and Sid helped Ethel to the door. There was an exchange of knowing smiles between Sid and Helen who he wasn't used to seeing standing up. She was quite a striking girl he thought who could do better with herself.

'Are you okay mum' she asked as Ethel shuffled awkwardly out of the house 'your eyes look all red and puffy.'

'Yes I'm okay, I just got a bit emotional talking to Sid about the old days.'

'You old softy, it doesn't take much to get you sniffing does it? Come on let me take you home I don't want you upsetting Mr Saines.'

Ethel smiled at Sid as she gingerly got into the car. 'Thank you' she whispered.

For his part Sid said he hoped to see her again soon, to which Ethel responded that he should call round when he was in that part of town.

Helen however didn't have to make that offer, she knew he would be calling round to see her sooner rather than later.

That evening, as Sid got into bed, he thought about the day's happenings and where his recent neighbour might now be residing and what he would say to Ethel next time they met. It was with these thoughts and the suggestion by WPC Charnley that he should see about getting a security chain fitted to his door that Sid slipped into a deep sleep.

Chapter 7

M onday morning dawned all too quickly for Sid who felt that the excitement of the last few days had made him deserving of a few more hours in bed. But, as a creature of habit, at 8 am he got up, made his breakfast, listened to the news on the local radio station and turned it off again as soon as the regular music came back on. He could remember his two children having pop music on in the house during the sixties when they were living at home and of an age to help determine what was heard in the house. At that time it was all longhaired layabouts who needed a good wash and a hard day's work. He didn't think that things had improved over the intervening 40 years except what pictures he had seen in the Daily Mirror did seem to show that at least they had their hair cut these days! He wasn't sure about washing or the work ethic though.

After washing his breakfast plates, and himself, in that order, Sid put on his coat and hat and set forth on the well-trodden path to the Council offices.

As Sid walked into the Housing Department offices he was surprised to see a man sitting in what he considered was Miss Treacher's seat.

'Good Morning' said the new incumbent.

'Good morning Mr err Terry' said Sid straining to read the man's identification badge.

'Nothing wrong with your eyes is there sir' replied the official clearly not realising to whom he was addressing.

'And I hope there is nothing wrong with your ears young man and that you will listen to what I have to say.'

At this point the smile faded from John Terry's face.

'Where is Miss Treacher?' asked Sid in a less menacing tone.

'Oh, she's on leave this week. Gone skiing in Andorra I believe.'

'Ain't that where rabbits come from?' enquired Sid trying to be knowledgeable.

'I wouldn't know sir. What can we do to help you, are you one of our tenants.'

'I've been one of your tenants, or your predecessors, the old borough council since 1954. I should be getting a long service or long suffering medal from the mayor soon.'

'Oh I see sir, well may I have your name and address and nature of your inquiry please?'

Sid then set out, in what he considered to be the simplest possible terms, what the WPC had said to him and how he would like to have a security chain fitted to his front door.

'There is a form to fill in for this sir' he was told.

'I thought there might be, well give it to me and I will see what I can do.'

After about ten minutes Sid appeared at the desk of Mr

Terry.

'Are you trying to take the piss?'

John Terry, who was a trainee recently graduated from the University of East Anglia and spending 6 weeks in each of the council's administrative departments, was not used to this type of forthright language, today being his first day in housing.

'What's the problem sir?'

'This bloody question 5.'

'For what purpose is the work required?'

'Well what is the work for sir?'

'To keep blood burglars out of course, what else would a security chain be needed for? Fixing to me cistern in the toilet maybe, or as an ankle chain!'

'You don't understand Mr Saines, the form you have is a ubiquitous one that encompasses a wide variety of requests and relates to incidental work to be carried out on one of our properties, excluding structural and general maintenance.'

'Oh well then why do you need all of this information? Any disability I might have, earnings and benefits received. You've got all of this on your files. I pay my rent every fortnight without fail, do you want to see my rent book?'

'No sir, I am sure you do but in order to help our administration we need you to fill this information out on this particular application form.'

After further deep mutterings Sid capitulated and completed the form and handed it over to Mr Terry.

'Thank you sir, this will now be processed by our works

maintenance section in conjunction with the Treasurer's Department who will determine the level of payment required for the work.'

'Payment' exclaimed Sid. 'It's a council house. I shouldn't have to pay.'

'Well sir' replied Mr Terry, 'its not part of the regular maintenance on the property or a replacement for fair wear and tear so strictly speaking we should charge for both parts and labour. However, let me see if I can get any further guidance on this matter from a senior housing officer.'

'Get Miss Johnson to come down' said Sid. 'Give her something to do.'

'I am sorry' said John, 'I don't think this is a matter that warrants her attention and besides she's not in today.'

Typical, thought Sid, bet her having to turn out on Saturday was a shock to her system and that she's had to have the day off to get over it.

Richard Gander was a tall slim thirty something member of the Housing Department. In terms of status he was third in seniority to Miss Johnson and so Sidney thought he was dealing with someone at least with some authority and he was male.

They sat down on the plastic chairs that "left a rigid impression on your arse" as Sid so eloquently put it, and began to discuss the background to Sid's request and what the WPC had said to him. If there was one thing that Sid enjoyed it was a good talk to anyone who would listen and Mr Gander was a good listener. At the end of the diatribe, which had been very much a one-way conversation, Mr Gander stood up and said 'Well I believe Mr Saines you have a legitimate case and we at Creekleigh District Council don't want our senior citizens to feel that they are in any way neglected or left unprotected when we have the ability to prevent that. I will arrange for you to have a security lock fitted within the next seven days and free of charge. A letter of confirmation for this will be sent to you and I will also contact the maintenance section and ask them to timetable you and make contact to arrange a mutual date and time. Sid shook Mr Gander's hand smiled at the 'new boy' on the front desk and walked home pleased with his mornings work.

He had just entered his house when the telephone rang. Sid answered it hesitantly as was his way. He had been connected for the last 15 years but he still felt uneasy about using it.

'Yes' he quietly spoke into the receiver.

'Mr. Saines' said a female voice at the other end, 'we are not selling anything but we do have in you area this week...'

'Stop right there' said Sid, his voice changing from uncertainty to annoyance, 'is this call about double glazing?'

'Well sir' came the uncertain reply 'we do supply secondary windows.'

'I don't want it, nor do I want the gas board to supply my electricity or the electric light company (as he always referred to them) to give me a bloody telephone line. Besides' said Sid 'this is a council house.'

'Can I take it that you are not interested in one of our local operators calling on you sir.' Sid did not give the call centre girl the courtesy of a reply he just slammed down the phone uttering expletives as he did so.

Double glazing salesmen, particularly those that use the

telephone for cold calling were one of Sid's pet hates. He recalled that when he used to live in the first floor maisonette almost opposite his bungalow about 15 years ago, before he retired from the garage, he received just such a call but from a man insistent that he should reap the benefits of double glazing. At that time Sid had informed the caller very politely but firmly that he lived in a council house but the caller was insistent that grants were available for people to improve rented accommodation and that he should consider the benefits for his family. Sid had explained he couldn't afford whatever special offer was available that particular week in the area and that the company should look elsewhere.

He remembered that they were particularly forceful in their marketing technique and insisted that if he only met their local representative he would see the benefits. Sid then tried to explain that his windows didn't need replacing at which point the caller changed his approach to wax lyrical about UPVC patio doors. The conversation had concluded with the caller saying that their representative would be in the area the next afternoon and would he be available?

'I won't be in until after 6' had been Sid's response hoping that this would put off the impending visit. Unfortunately, that had been acceptable to the rep and with that Sid's call had ended.

Sid recollected that soon after the conversation he forgot all about it, but that was until the following evening. As he had cycled round the corner of the road near to his home there had been an unfamiliar car parked outside his house and a man with a clip board pacing up and down looking extremely vexed.

As Sid pushed his bike up the garden path the man had

called over the fence to him 'Mr Saines?'

'Yes.'

'Mr Saines of number 30?'

'Yes.'

'Your property is on the first floor isn't it?'

'Yes.'

'My company office said you wanted a patio door. Are you taking the piss?'

'No' replied Sid 'you started it.'

At that point he put his bike into the shed, walked up his steps into his home and closed the door. However, he couldn't resist a peek around his curtains as he entered his front room and was just in time to see a Ford Escort roar away from the kerbside. As he had watched him disappear in a cloud of burning oil Sid had thought to himself perhaps they will listen next time, but numerous phone calls later confirmed to Sid that they, and their competitors, haven't.

Tuesday morning arrived and with it a call from the Council confirming that, if it was convenient the security chains would be fitted later that very day, probably sometime after lunch. Sid confirmed that this was acceptable and awaited the arrival of one of the councils finest a Mr Tom Croft who duly arrived at 2:15 much to Sid's surprise and delight. After he had introduced himself Sid said he thought he recognised the name and likewise Tom said he knew Sid as the father of an old school colleague Mark Saines, Sid's son.

They exchanged pleasantries about what Mark was doing now and where he lived while he fitted the security chain to the front door. Tom then asked if Sid wanted a similar fixture on the backdoor as his instructions from the council were to secure the outside door of the property. So Sid thought that it was a good idea as he had not got to pay and so Tom duly obliged. The entire operation was completed within 40 minutes and Sid signed Tom's work sheet to confirm that the work had been carried out and that he was satisfied with it. The council employee duly departed, after an exchange of remember me to Mark, and thank you for the neat and quick job. That was that thought Sid but he was to be mistaken.

Two days later as the letters fell onto Sid's 'Welcome' mat he picked up the usual array of envelopes. Readers Digest had confirmed that he had been selected for the next round in their special draw and that he had already won a prize that was just waiting to be claimed. All he had to do was return the envelope and agree to receive, on 21 days free trial, a copy of their latest book on Home Improvement Techniques. I've got a lot of use for one of those thought Sid and besides, as far as the free gift is concerned, I'm old enough to know you never get anything in this life for nothing.

This was to be prophetic as he opened a letter from the Council's Treasurers Department containing an invoice for £25 for the fitting of security chains at his property.

Sid went purple with rage 'those two faced bastards' he shouted to no one as his house was empty at the time. 'How dare they charge me, after all their promises. We'll see about this.'

The district council's treasurer's department was relatively new territory to Sid whose normal point of contract was through the housing department and so he was not too familiar with the layout of the department or their procedures.

On entering the main reception of the treasurer's department Sid was surprised at the level of decor and what he thought was opulence of the surroundings compared to that of the housing department.

Plastic chairs gave way to upholstered seating, there were small discreet rooms around the reception area where, he assumed, someone could discuss any problems without the world and his wife overhearing the conversation as in the open forum nature of the housing department. Instead of standing in a queue at the reception desk there was a ticket machine, like the one on the cheese counter at the local Tesco's thought Sid, that ensured a first come, first served basis for attention. Sid duly took a ticket numbered 83 and was pleased to see, looking up at the digital display screen, that number 81 was currently being attended to.

After about 5 minutes waiting Sid's number was flashed up and he approached the information desk.

'Good morning, my name is Sidney Saines of No. 9 The Avenue.'

Sid was not known personally within the Treasurers Department but his fame was.

'Oh yes Mr Saines' replied the girl behind the counter, 'and how can we help you'.

'You can help by explaining this' replied Sid almost slamming his offending letter on the desktop.

'Oh' exclaimed the receptionist again. 'Is there something wrong? Have you come to pay or query an account?'

'Query it!' gasped Sid. 'I certainly have.'

He then proceeded to explain, with the minimal amount of expletives, apologising each time he used one that it wasn't personal, his conversation with Mr Gander of the councils housing department.

'Well we appear to have a problem' he was told. 'I will see if someone in our accounts section can help. Would you care to go to room 2 over by the window and I will try to get someone to come and talk to you about it.'

Sid did as he was bid and after about a ten-minute wait the door of the little room opened and in strode a man who's identification badge revealed that he was Jeffrey Thomas, Section Leader Accounts.

'Now, what's the problem Mr Saines?'

'I've already explained to the young girl out there' said Sid gesticulating towards the door.

'I believe you were under the impression that the work carried out on your property for a security chain fitting was free of charge.'

'I wasn't under any impression' shouted Sid exasperated by this approach 'I was told it was.'

'Ah yes, Mr Gander of the housing department. Well Mr Saines, he was correct insofar as we were happy to fit the security chains as he said but you still have to pay for the chains themselves.'

'What!' shouted Sid, at which point everyone in the waiting room turned to stare at the small interview room containing the two men.

'You load of twisters.'

'No, no, no, this is an approved Council policy.'

'Approved by who?'

'The Finance Committee.'

Sid stood speechless for a moment and then said 'Well I can't afford this. I will go home and remove them myself and bring your bloody chains back to you. I think this is scandalous and I believe the local paper will agree with me on that.'

Oh dear thought Mr Thomas, we appear to have touched a nerve here.

The local elections were soon to be held and whilst as an officer of the council Mr Thomas had to remain impartial he was well aware of the implications that this type of publicity could have for the Council and more particularly his pending promotion to Assistant District Treasurer.

'Now, Mr Saines, we don't want to do that do we. I am sure we can arrive at some form of compromise.'

'Certainly we can. You either withdraw your invoice or you can have the chains back and I go and chat to the local paper. The bloke that writes about the weddings and the gardening column is an old mate of mine I am sure he will be keen on a 'human interest story.'

Whilst the argument was only over £25 Sid felt a principle was at stake here and that he had been conned by the Council. For his part Jeff Thomas realised that he had to act decisively or risk the wrath of both his superiors and the ward councillor if the matter got into the local paper, and finally, and not least, that of Sid Saines.

'Well' said Mr Thomas 'There is clearly a misunderstanding surrounding the work and as a long standing tenant I believe, in this instance, we can waive our normal charging procedures.'

'Oh right' said Sid who had been expecting a bit of a fight. 'So what are you going to do about it so that I don't get any more bloody bills from you.'

Jeff Thomas took the copy of the invoice that Sid had been clasping in his hand and wrote across it "cancelled."

'Please wait here Mr Saines, I just need to get this verified by accounts, I won't keep you long'.

As Sid watched the council official leave the room he began to take more notice of his surroundings. The room was relatively small with a table in the centre and four soft upholstered chairs set out around it. There were no windows but Sid could see, as he looked up, vents in the ceiling which he thought must be for air conditioning or something to get air into and out of the enclosed room. The walls were painted a pale magnolia with a single large picture on the wall opposite to where he was sitting that looked to him as if it had been painted out of focus with coloured blobs on a pale blue background. Sid got out of his seat and approached the picture. In the bottom right hand corner he read "Monet". Never heard of him thought Sid, probably some local painter the council got a job lot from on the cheap or else, knowing this lot of spendthrifts on their own creature comforts, some foreigner they commissioned to do the work at an exorbitant cost.

Sid returned to his seat and tilted it back against the wall onto the dado-rail that ran all around the room. This was a habit he had had since a child at the back of the classroom at Church Street Primary School. As he laid back wondering where the hell Mr Thomas had got to he heard a loud commotion outside of his room, but before he could adjust his chair position to go and investigate the door crashed open and in the doorway stood a large red faced man in a dark uniform with an Alsatian on a chain at his side.

'What the....' Sid's words were cut short by the burly intruder, who demanded to know, 'what's the problem?'

'What do you mean, what's the problem' retorted Sid keeping a close eye on the dog that was straining at its leash and creating a sticky pool of saliva on the carpeted floor of the interview room.

'The panic button's been pushed and the light outside of this room signifies that it happened here.'

'There's no other bugger in here but me' explained Sid now becoming more aggressive as he lost his own initial sense of alarm. 'I ain't pressed anything'.

The security guard stared at Sid. He was a large man, in his middle fifties Sid thought, with small piggy eyes and a uniform that was either too small for him originally or he had put on a considerable amount of weight since becoming fitted. The dog, which Sid was later to find out, was called Satan, also appeared overweight or was just a bloody big dog.

It was during this commotion that Mr Thomas returned. He squeezed past the security man, who was still standing in the doorway, as if to ensure that no one should leave the room for which his ample frame was well suited.

'Now then James, what going on here'

He don't look like a James to me thought Sid, more like a Charlie or a Ron.

'Well it's like this Mr Thomas' responded James. 'Someone in here pressed the panic button. As you know part of my duties are to respond to this. However, by the time I got here there was only this bloke in the room, I was a bit delayed though as I was walking the grounds at the time and so as the problem was up here on the first floor I had to wait for the lift. This is on account as you know, |I don't do stairs and Satan has this phobia about the oil painting of the mayor on the stairs landing.'

Sid felt he had remained silent for too long.

'I don't know what your problem is mate' raged Sid looking into the piggy eyes of James, 'but there has only been me in this room for the last ten minutes and I ain't pressed no panic buttons.'

'There is no button exactly in this room Mr Saines' interjected Mr Thomas.

'You see the dado rail around the room?'

'Yes'

'Well, that contains a touch sensitive strip. You see we occasionally have members of the public in here for interviews on sensitive business and it has been known for these to get out of hand and for council staff to be physically threatened. For this reason we have, what we like to call, a discreet alarm system whereby we can summons assistance from any part of the interview room.'

It then began to dawn on Sid that it must have been his antics of leaning back on his chair that had triggered the alarm and summoned the arrival of James the Security man.

'Seems that it must have been me after all' said Sid. 'Sorry to have caused any problems but how was I to know you had the bloody room booby-trapped?'

'No harm done' responded Mr Thomas. 'Thank you James for your attendance but you can see in this instance that you and Satan are not needed.'

James grunted. Satan let one more globule of saliva fall onto the carpet and then they both turned and departed.

'Sorry about all that Mr Saines, now where are we. Ah yes the question of your account. '

He then asked Sid to follow him to the cash desk adjacent to the information desk and spoke through the glass partition to the young girl sitting behind it.

'Carol' he said 'Can you please arrange to have this invoice formally cancelled, with the £25 replaced with a "no charge entry".'

'Certainly Mr Thomas' she replied and tapped at her keyboard with the result that a new invoice was generated which confirmed that there was no charge to the recipient of the work. Jeff Thomas handed the top copy to Sid and said he hoped that the matter had been successfully resolved and apologised for any misunderstanding.

As Sid left he looked around at the reception area of the treasurers department. He thought to himself its poor buggers like me who don't fight for their rights that have probably helped to pay for this lot.

Sid walked back to his bungalow thinking about the morning's events and how he considered he was hard done by. He recalled that he had always paid his rent on time, never been unemployed since starting work on the farm at the age of 14 and kept his house in good nick. Yet he had to fight to get what he considered was owed to him. If I had been an unmarried mother there would have been no question of me having to pay he thought. They just have to get themselves pregnant and the bloody authorities are falling over themselves to offer them a council house, subsidised rent and the place decorated from top to bottom.

Sid recalled his days in the maisonette where he and his wife had lived. When they had first moved in there had been an elderly couple living below them who, as Sid would say, kept themselves to themselves. But as the years passed they both became increasingly inactive and dependant on daily visits by nursing staff until a point was reached when they had to move out into a nursing home. Their premises had then remained vacant for a couple of months whilst various structural works were carried out including central heating being installed, which Sid's property did not have.

Then one morning Sid had observed what he considered was a young girl carrying a baby get out of the front of a large white van accompanied by a tall man with a shaven head and tattoo's on his forearms. The woman went into the house with the child and the man began unloading the van.

'Do you see that' Sid had said to his wife. 'We're going to have bloody screaming kids downstairs. They have given the flat to a young family.'

Little had he realised then that the young family turned out to be an unmarried mother with a three-month-old girl and an unemployed boyfriend. A lethal cocktail, as far as Sid's prejudices were concerned.

Over the next few weeks all Sid's concerns came to fruition with the baby crying at night and pop music being played loudly from dawn to dusk. The boyfriend, as Sid had now deduced he was and not the husband, was an irregular caller but on the nights he stayed Sid was disturbed in more ways than one as he morally disapproved of cohabiting and the moaning and banging of what he assumed was the headboard of the bed on the paper thin wall which kept him awake.

The bloke must be on Duracell's he had thought to himself one night when the action below him was even more torrid than usual. His wife had lain beside him thinking that Sid had never made her headboard thump as long or as loud as that.

Anyway, thought Sid as he arrived back from the council offices and admired his chain on the front door. I've got something out of the buggers today.

Chapter 8

That evening as Sid sat by his gas fire sucking his pipe of Old Holborn and watching The Bill, his favourite television program (alongside Brookside), he felt his eyes becoming heavy.

Too early to go to bed yet he thought but maybe I'll have forty winks before the Nine O'clock News. So he took his pipe from his mouth, which he thought had burnt it's self out, and placed it into the trouser pocket of his tracksuit bottoms. Not that Sid was in anyway sporting but he found them comfortable for sitting around the house in.

Sid soon slipped into a deep sleep but was awakened by the smoke detector on his lounge wall beeping loudly and a disembodied voice saying 'Are you alright Mr Saines, please respond?'

Sid awoke to a pain on his right side and an acrid smell of burning. He looked down to see a large hole in his trousers that were both smoking and melting with the heat from the pipe he had placed in his pocket.

Sid leapt to his feet and almost fell into the bathroom where he turned the showerhead from the baths mixer taps onto the smouldering area. Fortunately there did not appear to be any serious damage to his leg only a large red area.

Whilst the smoke detector had, by this time, ceased its beeping there was still the voice on the intercom in the lounge becoming increasingly agitated.

'Mr Saines are you okay.' This is central control please respond.'

Sid walked gingerly back into the lounge and shouted at the microphone next to the relay device on his wall.

'Yeah, I'm okay, just forgot to put me pipe out'.

'Are you sure' asked a relieved yet still concerned voice.

'Sure, no harm done, except I need a new pair of trousers and to dry me pipe out.'

'All right then thank you' said central control 'Good night and please be more careful in future.'

'I will, good night'.

Sid spent a somewhat restless time in bed that night. The effect of the pipe burn on his thigh had been greater than he had first appreciated. After bidding the central controller goodnight he had gone to the bathroom to see what cream, ointment or lotion, he didn't care which, he might have that he could put on the inflamed red area to offer some soothing relief.

Sid had pills and potions for most things in his bathroom cabinet that he had collected over the years, most of which were well past their use or sell by date.

He unearthed bottles of tablets for which he had long forgotten what they had been prescribed to cure or protect against. There were medicines in bottles of various colours most of which had separated leaving a watery content sitting above a darker settled liquid below it.

There was, he knew, potions to make you go to the toilet and those to make you stop, both of which he had required in the past and had sought the advice of the old family doctor, Dr. Turner

Eventually at the back of the cupboard, Sid's hands alighted on a small brown screw top jar which had a faded label but from which Sid was just able to read the words 'Zinc and Castor Oil'. Sid was always careful in his food to check sell by dates, not so however when it came to the contents of his medicine cupboard.

Sid recalled that his wife had explained to him that it helped protect their babies' backsides from soreness that wet nappies could produce and also act as a soothing cream for their potentially sore parts. Well thought Sid; if its good enough for use on a baby it sure wont hurt my old arse.

Looking to see if there was a use by date on the label Sid drew a blank, probably because its manufacture predated the time when this practice became mandatory. Sid smoothed the cooling cream over the offending area with his old gnarled fingers and immediately felt some relief. He then replaced his pyjamas and went back to bed and slept fitfully until morning but regularly woke as he inadvertently turned onto the side of his burn. Bloody smoking he thought to himself it will be the death of me yet as he turned over again, carefully, and went back to sleep.

As Sid entered Dr. Turner's surgery he looked around the waiting room at the various array of local townsfolk sitting glumly on the plastic chairs each clutching a long piece of coloured Perspex on which was printed a number. The practice which Sid was registered with retained a total of four doctors, three male and one female the latter of whom Sid had consulted on occasions and found very efficient and he thought knowledgeable for a woman, but he preferred to trust in the old family doctor who he thought must be getting close to retirement age.

'Yes', snapped the archetypical receptionist behind the Formica topped counter.

'Is Doctor Turner available this morning' asked Sid politely.

'No' came the curt response. 'Have you got an appointment?'

'No I haven't' replied Sid already becoming annoyed with the woman's confrontational attitude.

'Well he could see you at, now let me see,' she said as she thumbed through a thick appointment book. 'Next Monday at 10:40.'

'That's no bloody good to me' replied Sid his voice becoming louder. People began to look up from the copies of Vanity Fair and Yachting Monthly, magazines they never read anywhere else.

'Well I am sorry he is not due back in the surgery until then as he is on holiday.'

Sid then remembered, of course, he was away in Northern Italy or was it Spain. Anyway he recalled from a conversation he had had about his garden that he would be away for a few days and that Sid had agreed to do some winter digging for him during that period and keep an eye on the greenhouse cacti.

'You should have made an appointment' the receptionist was saying as Sid stopped recalling his discussion with the doctor and concentrated on the immediate problem of getting medical assistance.

'Okay, well who can I see?'

'Do you have an appointment' Sid was again asked.

'Of course I don't have an appointment' shouted Sid becoming exasperated. 'If I'd had an appointment it would have been with Dr Turner, he is obviously not here and anyway another thing, I only hurt myself last night and didn't have the foresight to telephone you before I did it to make a bloody appointment.'

A series of giggles ran around the surgery waiting room as people sympathised with Sid's plight and the system whereby you have to know when you are going to be ill in order to see a doctor at a suitable time.

'No need to raise your voice sir' replied the receptionist who had had years of experiencing this type of reaction from the patients she saw on a daily basis.

'Is your case urgent.'

'Course it is, I'm in bloody pain.'

'All right' responded the dragon as Sid referred to her.

'Name.'

At last thought Sid. He gave her his name and address and after searching through a large filing cabinet the receptionist emerged with a buff wallet type file.

'Well Mr Saines, Dr Roberts should be able to see you at the end of her appointments.

'That's the lady doctor isn't it' said Sid warily.

'Yes, is that a problem for you?'

'Err no, but aren't any of the male doctors available?'

'No I am afraid if you want to see a doctor today it's Dr. Roberts or no one.'

At which point Sid took the yellow plastic card he had been given and walked to one of the few spare chairs in the waiting room and sat down between a woman of ample girth with thick bandages around the bottom of her legs and a young woman with a child of about 5 or 6 years old Sid thought. He sat on the plastic seat for a while looking around the waiting room. The woman with bandages beside him looked at Sid and smiled and spoke softly.

'Well done, that receptionist over there needed someone to say something to her. It's us what pays her wages through our national insurance isn't it.'

'Yeah' replied Sid who felt more intimidated by the size and bulk of the woman sitting beside him than he had by the officious attitude of the dragon.

Sid began to muse. I wonder what's wrong with her legs. Maybe her ankles have given up carrying her around. Suddenly Sid felt a sharp pain in his thigh. The little boy next to him had rammed the space ship he had been pushing up and down the adjoining chair straight into his affected spot causing Sid audibly to wince.

'Oh I am sorry' said the woman who Sid took to be the mother of the little hooligan. He had quickly formed an opinion of the child soon after he had sat down as he could see the presence of an earring and that it was being worn by a boy! Sid thought that was reprehensible. He had also noted that the assumed mother had a tattoo that further helped to alienate Sid from the couple.

'Okay' replied Sid, but don't let the little boy do it again please.'

'Tell the man you are sorry Tarquin.'

Tarquin, thought Sid, what sort of a name is that to go to bed with.

'Sorry mister my space ship was taking off and your leg just got in the way.'

Calm returned to the waiting room and for the first time Sid took a look at his piece of yellow plastic with the number 17 emblazoned on it. He then glanced up at the number currently against the yellow square on the side of the reception area. It said eight!

Eight thought Sid, Christ I'll be here all morning, still I've got to see someone about me leg. So, unusually for Sid, he settled down with a copy of House and Garden and waited while there was a coming and going into and out of the surgery, but gradually the numbers dwindled.

The large woman next to him was soon called for which Sid was grateful to get some additional space. But unfortunately the woman and her delinquent son on the other side were still there an hour later.

With the pain from the impact of Thunderbird 3 taking off now receding Sid, always one for conversation casually remarked to the mother 'Take their time here don't they'

'Yes, I couldn't help but overhear your conversation with the receptionist, we also didn't have an appointment but my son's condition only appeared last night so I thought I must take him to the doctors this morning to get it treated.'

'Oh I hope it's nothing serious' said Sid as he playfully ruffled the young lads hair.

'Well I think its probably chicken pox.'

It was five minutes to twelve when Sid finally got into the consulting room of Dr. Roberts.

'Sorry to keep you waiting Mr Saines, how can I help you?'

'Well you see doctor' said Sid as he outlined the events of the previous evening.

'Dear dear, well lets have a look at you then.'

Sid gingerly lowered his trousers and lifted up the side of his underpants to reveal the large red patch, the result of hot Old Holborn against skin.

'My my that does look sore'

Sid explained his use of zinc and castor oil and that it had helped soothe the initial pain but that he was concerned that he was doing the right thing.

'You probably did the right thing' explained the doctor who advised that it should be dressed and that she would supply some further cream to help reduce the soreness.

'The nurse will dress it for you she said, please put your trousers back on. 'She again apologised for the length of time Sid had had to wait and took him into the dispensary for the nurse to carry out the necessary first aid.

As a pensioner and on supplementary benefit Sid did not have to pay for the prescription.

That pleased him a lot. You get bugger all now a days that's free he thought as the nurse gently rubbed a yellowish coloured cream into his thigh and then covered it with large wadding and taped it to his upper leg.

'Come back in a couple of days' said the nurse 'and well see how it's progressing and you won't need an appointment.'

She had also heard the fracas caused by Sid on his arrival at the surgery.

Sid arrived home and made a note on his wall calendar to visit the surgery the day after tomorrow, he also then saw the note he had made for himself that the same day he should visit Dr. Turner's house to check on the greenhouse and do a bit of winter digging.

I should have read that this morning he thought to himself. It might have saved a bit of the confusion and argument down at the surgery with the old battleaxe behind the counter.

Two days later Sid was back at the doctors. The treatment he had had on his leg had certainly eased his discomfort and he told the nurse so. She duly changed the dressing and said that he could remove it himself, say at the weekend, but that to be careful when bathing.

Sid was always a careful bather he did it once a week, usually on a Sunday night when he would put his emersion heater on long enough to get a bath full of hot water. Not that he didn't wash himself during the week but baths were a once a week event.

Chapter 9

On leaving the surgery Sid headed off across town to the home of Dr. Turner. The morning was dry and bright but there was a winter's crispness in the air enhanced by the wind from the Irish Sea.

Sid arrived at the house, entering as usual by the side gate. The dwelling was large with well kept front borders, thanks mainly to Sid's endeavours, with a large vegetable patch, lawn and small orchard to the rear. Sid estimated it probably had 4 or 5 bedrooms but he had only been into the kitchen of the house when invited in for elevenses or an afternoon cup of tea by the doctor or his wife. Sid liked both of them but their association was one very much like the characters Ted and Ralph from the Fast Show. Sid, whilst a proud man, was also conscious of his status in society and saw a professionally educated man like the doctor and his wife as being of a different order to himself. Again, as with another analogy from the famous John Cleese, Ronnie Barker and Ronnie Corbet comedy sketch from the early sixties he looked up to both of them "as he knew his place."

Sid was just opening the shed door to retrieve his fork,

spade and wheelbarrow when he was startled by a voice behind him

'Hello Sid' said the familiar voice. Turning around Sid saw Mrs Turner standing in front of him.

'Oh hello, you startled me, I didn't think there was anyone here, I thought you and the doctor had gone off to the sun for a week.'

'Well Donald has but I have stayed behind to clear up a few things before leaving.'

'Oh so you're going later'

'No I'm afraid not Sid. I mean that I am leaving, we are going our separate ways.'

Still Sid did not fully grasp the situation.

'Me and my wife often thought about separate holidays but we never did, suppose it had something to do with the bloody single supplement the hotels always put on lone travellers.'

'You're not understanding me Sid. Donald and I are to get a divorce.'

Sid stood with his spade in his hand speechless. He had always considered the two a happily married couple and whilst he had never been close to either of them socially he believed that he was a good judge of character and that in the case of the Turner's he could not comprehend what he had just been told.

Eventually Sid responded by saying 'What, you and the doctor splitting up.'

'I'm afraid so Sid. Donald is on holiday with his friend in Spain and I will be living in London from now on. Donald will be staying on here and I am sure he will still be grateful for your services Sid but no doubt he will talk to you about it next week. Now I am sure you've things to do, I attended to the cacti so you need not bother about them. I've got to go and sort out some things in the house. If you would like to call round the kitchen about 3 0'clock I will have a cup of tea waiting.'

At that she turned round and went back into the house leaving Sid still trying to come to terms with what he had just heard. He had always thought the doctor and his wife had the perfect family. They had two sons who Sid had seen grow up, or at least from the age of their early teens, and whenever he had seen the couple together they seemed like any normal pair. They occasionally argued, well what couple didn't, thought Sid recalling his married life.

But for them to split up! Still, he thought, at least there are no young kids involved with both sons now being away at university. One at Durham he thought studying to be a vet with the other in some unpronounceable town in Wales studying town planning. Now there is a useful subject he thought!

Anyway this isn't getting the winter digging done thought Sid and with these winter days you don't get very long afternoons and before you know it your digging in the dark. So Sid set to work with his trusty spade but as 3pm came round he put down his tools and walked slowly up to the kitchen and tapped on the door.

'Come in' he heard through the door.

Sid removed his Wellington boots at the threshold before entering the house. The room was large; Sid estimated it was about the size of his little bungalow if you took away the hall and bathroom. The kitchen was warm and inviting. Stella Turner was in the corner of the room with an ironing board.

'Must just get these things pressed before I put them in the suitcases. I'll be with you in a minute or two'

'No hurry Mrs Turner' said Sid 'I think I have finished for the day, anyway its beginning to rain and there will be no point in me continuing in that given the nature of your soil.'

She finished the ironing, placed the board in the utility cupboard in the corner of the room and proceeded to get two mugs from off the huge Welsh dresser that dominated one wall of the kitchen. She knew of old that

Sid felt happier with a mug than a cup and saucer and was happy to join him with one.

She pushed a saucer of biscuits towards Sid who soon devoured all of them except for the Garibaldi's. Can't abide those he thought to himself, the black bits get under the top plate of me dentures.

Stella filled the cups with strong PG Tips from the teapot and invited Sid to add milk and sugar. Always put the milk in first myself, thought Sid, but maybe this is the posh way to do it. His hostess then sat down opposite Sid, her sharply chiselled features looking rather drawn Sid thought but whose wouldn't be that way if your husband was in a foreign country with another woman and you were left alone in the family home.

He had never really got to know Stella Turner as his main contact had been through her husband the doctor with whom he had the most discussions about the garden, weather and sometimes out of surgery hours his minor ailments and afflictions.

Unusually for Sid he felt a little awkward about his current situation insofar as he felt he was imposing on someone else's grief.

'Have you somewhere fixed up to stay' asked Sid not meaning to be inquisitive but more through concern.

'Yes Sid, I am flat hunting at the moment but for the next few days I'll be staying with a work colleague at his house until I get myself sorted out.

We thought it best that I should make my departure while Donald was away. We will sort out furniture and other matters once I have a permanent base.'

Staying at his house thought Sid, bugger me she's at it as well, still I suppose what's good for the goose as they say.

Sid drank the rest of his tea and bade his farewell.

'Donald will settle up with you at the end of the month as usual' she called out as Sid left 'Look after yourself.'

'And you' replied Sid putting on his Wellingtons and walking back up the garden path towards the town and home.

For her part Stella opened the kitchen window as even though it brought an icy draft into the kitchen it helped remove the stale odour of Sid's socks that had been in an uncovered state within feet of her for the best part of the last fifteen minutes. I should have had a word with Donald about Sid's feet I'm sure he could have prescribed something even if it was only soap she thought.

As Sid walked home the lights of the town were twinkling and the rain had become more intense but he was too preoccupied with his thoughts to issue his general expletives about the winter weather. For a gardener, Sid had a strong aversion to rain.

It was the following week before Sid returned to the doctor's residence; the burn on his side had reseeded into little more than a minor irritation although the affected area was clearly visible.

Obviously, thought Sid, the doctor's wife must have told him of his work last week as he had found an envelope had been pushed through his letterbox late on Monday evening with a ten pound note and a request for him, if he was available and that the weather was favourable, for his services on Wednesday.

As usual Sid went round to the rear of the property and knocked at the kitchen door. A bronzed looking doctor who invited Sid into the now familiar kitchen opened it.

'Thanks for coming round Sid, I am anxious this year to make a real show with the garden and increase the vegetable crop and so we need to try to get as much preparation work done as we can. I don't expect you to dig it all by hand yourself so I have hired a rotavator, but it still needs someone who understands gardening to get the soil ready'.

'Well' replied Sid 'I'll have a go'.

'You and me both' replied the doctor.

Sid soon found that using a rotavator was very much like a petrol driven mower he used on the doctors front garden and whilst he was pleased with the area of ground he was able to cover in a relatively short time he was less pleased at the results in terms of quality digging. It's not the same thought Sid, as with a good spade and a deep spit.

71

It was beginning to get dark and so Sid thought that as there was not a light on the bloody rotavator that he ought to pack up for the day. He had unfortunately waited in vain for a call that a cup of tea was waiting and the doctor's initial interest in the rotavator had been short lived.

Sid cleaned up the blades of the machine, closed off the petrol and pushed it into the gathering gloom of the shed. As he prepared to leave the doctor suddenly appeared at the doorway of the kitchen, it's florescent light highlighting his tall frame in the door.

'Oh, thanks Sid, didn't realise it was so late'.

The glow from the kitchen fell across part of the area Sid had just been rotavating.

'Looks good Sid, William and I are looking forward to the spring and summer vegetables already'.

William! Thought Sid, who the hell is William, certainly not his sons, although he couldn't actually recall their names at that present moment and it's not the cat or the dogs thought Sid who he knew were called C4 and Tyson.

"See for Cat" had taken a while for Sid to understand and Tyson the Jack Russell Sid thought was a vicious little sod.

'You haven't met William have you? William can you spare me a moment please.'

As he appeared in the open doorway Sid could see he was younger than the doctor albeit not by many years, he was smaller in height and stature but had blonde hair and steely blue eyes.

'William, meet Sid, more a family friend than a gardener.'

Sid held out a muddy hand.

'Sorry about the dirt' he said.

'That's okay Sid' replied William in what Sid took to be a strong northern dialect 'Nice to meet you'.

'William will be living here for a while and so don't be alarmed if you see him around the place and I am not about.'

'Oh, right' said Sid a little bewildered by the turn of events.

William turned and walked back into the house leaving the doctor and Sid on the doorstep together.

'I understand my wife explained to you about us going our separate ways and I am sure you will be discreet in what you know'

'Oh yeah, sure.'

'There is nothing secret about what has happened but, well you know William and I have known each other for a number of years and well on holiday in Spain' the doctor's voice suddenly tailed off. 'Anyway Sid I am sure I don't have to spell it out to a man of the world like you. See you next week and I will pop the money round as usual later in the week. If you feel up to it I would appreciate the digging, or should I say rotavating, being done as soon as possible but I understand your other commitments and that none of us are getting any younger. Bye Sid' and with that he closed the door leaving Sid in the dark but very much enlightened over other issues.

That night as Sid sat eating his evening meal in his small lounge whilst watching The Bill he tried to pull together the strands of what he liked to call the doctors affair. Had his wife left him for another man? Whose house she now residing in or was she an innocent party?

Then there was the even bigger conundrum of the doctor and his male friend. He can't be gay thought Sid, he has a couple of kids and been married for twenty odd years, or can he?

Sid then began to think of the ramifications of his conclusion. If he is gay thought Sid, then, as he has been my GP for ages that don't seem right. Sid tried to search back in his memory banks for any event or conversation he might have had with the doctor that was relevant to his new found knowledge but try as he might he couldn't. Well if he is gay then he has kept it bloody quiet thought Sid as he stood in his kitchen washing up his dinner plates and looking out into the darkness that was his winter garden.

Chapter 10

In recent years it had been Sid's normal experience to wear a pair of track suit bottoms to lounge around in the evening but his experience with the pipe in his pocket and the effect of melting lycra on his skin had led to a change in his attire. As a result of that he was wearing a pair of casual lightweight trousers on this particular evening.

During a break for advertising in The Bill, Sid briskly walked across his lounge and into the bathroom having waited for a natural break to relieve himself. However in his hurry to return to the TV set as he heard the incidental music starting he quickly raised the zip fly only to get a part of his scrotum caught in it. The pain seared through Sid's body as he tried to extricate himself from the offending grip but he couldn't remove it and every movement he made appeared to make the pain more intense.

Christ, I need help thought Sid and for the first time in his warden controlled bungalow he pulled the red cord which was located in all three rooms of his house.

Almost immediately a voice from the speaker on the wall responded with an 'Are you all right Mr. err Saines.'

'No I am not ' responded Sid 'I've had a bit of an accident' at which point he let out a cry of pain. This had the effect of alarming the operator at central control who again asked

'What's wrong Mr Saines do you need assistance?'

'Yes, yes please' said Sid being unusually polite (albeit he was in an unusual predicament)

'I've caught me goolies, I mean me privates in my trouser zip'

'Are you able to extricate yourself' responded the male voice over the intercom system, which was able to sympathise with Sid's situation.

'No' winced Sid. 'Every time I touch the bloody zipper it hurts like hell.'

'Okay' replied the disembodied voice 'we will have someone with you as soon as possible.'

'Tell them to hurry up please.'

'They will be as quick as they can' he was assured.

After what seemed like an eternity to Sid, but was actually twenty minutes, Sid heard a vehicle stop outside his bungalow and moving back the curtain saw it was the white van of the paramedics. Sid painfully made his way to the front door and almost collapsed in pain as the young medical officer entered his house. He sat Sid down on the toilet seat in his bathroom and surveyed the damage.

'Oh nasty' he commented and gave Sid a local anaesthetic to help relieve the pain. He then broke the zip explaining that Sid was fortunate that it was only a nylon zip and not a metal one, given the situation Sid had got himself into as it would have been a hospital job.

At that moment he didn't care he was just grateful to have the offending fastener removed from his private parts.

With the zip removed the medic carried out an inspection of the damage it had created and administered some antiseptic lotion to the affected part and suggested that he might wish to accompany them back to the local accident and emergency unit for some further treatment.

Sid declined their offer, not being fully aware that the local anaesthetic effect had not yet worn off, but agreed that he would visit his local doctors' surgery next morning if he felt any discomfort. At this point his saviours, as he considered them to be, bade farewell and drove off into the night.

Sid sat on his bed. His nether regions throbbed as he thought to himself I will be a darned sight more careful in future. He put on a pair of loose fitting pyjamas and very gingerly got into bed. As he lay down he thought to himself what a blessing his alarm system was and what he would have done without it.

Next morning he awoke with a throbbing pain coming from "down below" and on closer inspection of the damage of the previous nights work he could see that the wound in his scrotum was weeping. Looks like I'm going to have to visit the quacks as they suggested he thought and so at 8:30 as the surgery opened Sid telephoned to try to get an appointment or better still a home visit. He couldn't face the prospect of sitting for hours on the plastic chairs in the waiting room. Whether or not he got another receptionist or the regular dragon was in a good mood he didn't know, but Sid tried to explain to her the events of the previous evening to which her response was.

'Oh you poor man I will put you on the doctors list for a

home visit today.

I know he is very busy but he should be with you by late morning.'

'Thank you' Sid replied as he replaced the handset.

Sid decided that despite his earlier problems with tracksuit bottoms and lighted pipes he would return to them in the interest of the comfort of his genitals and for ease of removal when the doctor arrived.

Better try to tidy up the lounge before the doctor arrives thought Sid who had been brought up with the idea that doctors expected a house to be spotlessly clean and tidy before they would consider entering it. But before he could start he heard the familiar mewing at the back door that he duly opened and in fell Fluff his old tabby tomcat.

'Morning Fluff' he said 'you missed an interesting night last night.'

The animal was as usual oblivious to Sid's conversation and sat mewing adjacent to the cupboard it now associated with containing its tins of food.

Sid opened the cupboard next to the sink to reveal a large selection of tins.

'Okay Fluff,' he said in the type of voice people seem to use for talking to animals.

'What flavour of Kit-e-Kat do you want today?'

The cat pushed its head into the cupboard and began rubbing its chin and whiskers around a tin. 'You silly bugger' said Sid 'they are giant marrow fat peas; here have this trout and salmon.'

Sid pulled the ring pull and placed some of the contents

into a china bowl with the description "DOG" written across it and placed the bowl on the floor by the back door.

Sid had bought the bowl cheap at a car boot sale and thought that as the cat couldn't read then what the heck. As he put the fleshy chunks into the bowl he thought this bloody cat eats better than me, when was the last time I had salmon for tea.

Fluff duly devoured the contents of the dog bowl and then proceeded to preen himself before heading off to the lounge and the front of the gas fire. What a life thought Sid, for Fluff was now his only companion. Both during and since his marriage Sid had always had a cat in the house. Didn't like dogs as he thought they were too much trouble having to walk them daily and groom them

A Heinz 57 cat, as he liked to refer to mongrel moggies, was much more his style. He also didn't like poncy names for his cats either. This was his fifth cat and all of them had been called Fluff, irrespective of their appearance, gender or length of coat. The current incumbent of the name was a shorthaired darkish shade of tabby. Having finished preening Fluff stretched out on the hearthrug and was soon sound asleep.

Bloody good ain't it thought Sid, what a life, as he went back gingerly to his housework in readiness for the doctor's visit.

About 11:30 Sid sat down carefully with his morning cup of coffee and digestive biscuit and it was then that the thought struck him. What if it's Dr Turner that comes!

In the past Sid would have been pleased to see him but events of the last few days had filled him with a degree of apprehension, particularly in this case, given the nature of his medical problem.

Christ thought Sid if he is "one of them", as he liked to colloquially put it, I ain't sure I want to show him me problem, it wouldn't be right. Then he thought, he hasn't suddenly changed his sexuality has he, he must have had tendencies for years. He then began to think back as to what ailments he had consulted Dr Turner on in the past.

Most of them, he concluded, were associated with stomach disorders, flu and various hand and arm injuries sustained at work in the garage. But he did recall the event of a couple of years ago that again had again involved injury to his private parts.

At that time he had been trying to hang up a couple of slate based etchings he had brought back from a holiday in North Wales and had gone out to his garden shed late one evening to retrieve a small hammer, as the one he had been trying to use had too large a head, and he had only succeeded in hitting his fingers holding the nail. On entering the shed it had been too dark to see clearly but Sid had dispensed with the idea of returning to the house for his torch as he was sure he could put his hands straight on the requisite tool. Unfortunately, as Sid had reached forward he upset a jam jar containing a paintbrush that he was soaking in turps. This emptied a mauve liquid down the front of his trousers soaking them, the underpants beneath and, from there his skin. As the liquid penetrated Sid could feel a burning sensation. Christ he thought I've got to get these clothes off. He turned quickly to get out of the shed banging his elbow on his bike and clattering a number of seed trays onto the floor. After finally stubbing his toe on something extremely hard Sid emerged into the twilight of his back garden disturbing Fluff, who had been until that point studying the movement of what he hoped was an unsuspecting mouse behind the water butt. But Sid's frantic movements had ensured that for the time being, at least, his prey had escaped.

Sid rushed into his bathroom removing his trousers and underpants as quickly as he could. He then stood in his bath and turned on the shower handset and directed the spray at his lower parts. The stinging sensation continued so Sid thought the best strategy was to try to wash all traces of the turps from his person. He then sat in the bath and as it gradually filled with warm water he carefully washed and soaped the affected area as vigorously as he dared.

Once he was satisfied that soap and water could do no more he had got out of the bath and padded himself dry with a clean towel from his airing cupboard. The next day he had visited Dr. Turner at his surgery concerned that he might have done some permanent damage to himself, and recalled vividly the doctor's response on seeing his predicament.

'Christ' said the doctor, 'it looks like a barber's pole' what have you been doing to yourself?'

The front doorbell rang, Sid had been so preoccupied in his thoughts he had not seen the car pull up outside or Dr. Roberts get out. On opening the door Sid didn't know whether to be relieved to see her instead of Dr Turner but he felt he needed medical attention and so he greeted her warmly and invited her into his lounge.

'Now what's the problem Mr Saines? I recall last time we met you had had a bit of an accident with your pipe. All healed up now?'

'Oh yeah' replied Sid

'So what appears to be the problem now, I understand

from the surgery that the paramedics had to offer you assistance last night and that you didn't feel capable of visiting the surgery today.'

Sid explained briefly the events of the previous evening.

'Oh you poor man' she responded.

How the hell can she understand, thought Sid, anyhow he was grateful for some sympathy as she examined his wound.

'Ohm, that is nasty. You should have taken the medics advice and gone to casualty.   I'll arrange for the district nurse to call and see you tomorrow. Meanwhile, I'll leave you this prescription for some cream. Make sure you keep it clean and apply the medication as instructed on the tube'.

'Yes doctor' replied Sid 'thank you for coming.'

Sid replaced his trousers and underpants and escorted Dr Roberts to the door.

'Goodbye' she said 'and please be more careful in future'

She smiled almost playfully and got into her car thinking to herself what is it with that bloke and his abuse of his lower parts.

Chapter 11

It wasn't until later that day that Sid glanced at the calendar on the kitchen wall and remembered that it was his wedding anniversary. This made him feel very melancholy, the watery winter sun outside was making way for a dark winter's night and as he let Fluff out he thought he detected flakes of snow in the air. Sid returned to his fireside and as he did so he opened the sideboard cupboard and removed the family photo album. So many memories he thought as he slowly turned the pages with the old sepia pictures of his parents and childhood slowly being overtaken by first monochrome and then coloured photos of his wife, children and now grandchildren.

Time, he thought is a funny thing as he began to realise that he could clearly recall events and situations of more than 50 years ago far more vividly than those of only a few weeks ago. He could remember his father telling him that his school days would be the happiest days of his life, devoid of worldly worries or concerns. He thought that he would like to have been able to tell his old man just how bloody wrong he had been. He had hated school and the teachers even more. There was, he recalled, one of the tales his father had told him of his school days that did not reflect well on his love of education either.

His father's story, the truth of which he was never able to confirm, was of how one morning at the small village school the school mistress, as she was known, had been excessively brutal with them both verbally and physically with the use of the dreaded strap. As a result he, Sid's father, and a couple of cohorts waited until she made her regular lunchtime visit to the school 'Thunder Box.' As there was no sewer in the village the toilet was a simple wooden shed with a bucket that was accessed for removal and emptying via a small low-level doorway at the rear of the wooden hut.

The three boys waited until they were sure she was well settled and then, with each of them armed with a handful of long nettles plucked with gloved hands from the adjacent field, they quietly opened the access door and as one they had thrust their pickings up and into the recesses of the hut. Sid's father claimed the screams and expletives that came from the thunder box were unimaginable and they made a very rapid retreat.

Unfortunately for the three lads another member of the small school staff observed their actions and as a result they were mercilessly caned for their misdemeanours. However, they later claimed that it was worth it.

Given his current level of discomfort Sid felt, as he recalled the story, a degree of pity for the unfortunate schoolmistress.

With his thoughts still on children Sid turned the page of the album where he was confronted with a picture of his two grandchildren then aged about 10 and 15 he would guess. At the time the photographs were taken his son and daughter-in-law lived relatively close and so were able to regularly visit him. On one such visit he vividly remembered trying to prepare what he considered to be a special treat for the kids, a jelly. It was normal, on these Sunday visits, that his visitors would provide all the food and simply use his kitchen to prepare it. However, on this occasion Sid had been to Budgens' and purchased some of their own-brand jelly. He had never made one before but thought well it must be simple enough. On opening the cardboard packaging he had read

"Place contents in a bowl and add a pint of boiling water. Stir briskly, wait until cool and place in a refrigerator."

Simple he had thought. He emptied the contents straight into a large bowl and boiled up a kettle of water. He found a calibrated jug and measured into it a pint of boiling water and poured it onto the jelly. He gave it a good stir and as instructed left it on his kitchen work surface. About an hour later he placed it into the refrigerator.

That evening Sid proudly unveiled his piece of culinary expertise with which he hoped to impress and please two would be grateful boys.

Teenage boys are not renowned for their love of jelly. However, they were wise enough to know that their grandad had taken, what was for him, a lot of trouble to produce the green shining bowl that was now before them and both admitted they would like some. It was as the youngest child ate his portion, Sid remembered with acute embarrassment, that the older one began to laugh uncontrollably while his brother looked anything but happy. As he ate there slowly emerged the cellophane wrapping that had encased the raw jelly. The instructions had said nothing about removing it and Sid had not realised that there had been a further wrapping to the jelly crystals apart from the outer cardboard. This event had gone down in family folklore and whilst Sid could grin at his mistake now he had not been so amused at the time.

He did however recall that the grandchildren had said that despite the wrapper the jelly had been nice. Such good boys he thought although they had caused him considerable embarrassment at other times. One day they had been visiting as usual and as they arrived he had been working in his old shed that was becoming increasingly damp due to the poor condition of the felt roof. They don't make felt like they used to. In the old days it would have stayed supple for years but now after only a few summers it becomes brittle and cracks. Probably imported from abroad he thought.

Whilst in his shed he showed the two boys some of his tools that his father had handed down to him but they appeared to show little interest in Victorian billhooks and snobs for cobbling. Peter had advised him that there was not a lot of call for homemade cobbling nowadays with so many people wearing trainers. They had also both pointed out that a lot of the tools looked dirty and were showing signs of rust, probably due to the dampness of the shed. Sid had explained to them that some of the items, particularly those with cutting edges, should be protected from rusting and that a film of grease was a good way of helping to achieve this. After this the conversation had tailed off as the boys became disinterested and wandered back into the house.

That afternoon Sid vividly remembered walking into the town with his son, daughter-in-law and two grandchildren and entering the local Superdrug store where he was a regular customer and well known to the staff. As often occurs on these group shopping expeditions the family got separated in the shop which was busy being a Saturday afternoon, but then suddenly Sid heard young Paul's voice ringing out

'Here's some Vaseline for your saw's granddad.'

Sid didn't go back into Superdrug for a couple of weeks after that event and when he finally did return he felt sure all of the staff were sniggering at him.

So many memories thought Sid as he continued to turn the pages of the album. Thoughts flooded through his mind of his life. The ups and downs and the good times especially those he had spent with his wife and how badly he missed her, particularly on the dark lonely winter evenings.

Their marriage had, in general, been a happy affair with both of them having to work to bring in a decent wage. As he looked at a photograph of her sitting in a deck chair, probably somewhere on the south coast, he couldn't recall exactly where, his thoughts turned to past holidays. They had had to save all year for a week or two away with the boys, normally at a holiday camp, where she could have a rest from the cooking and washing up and the kids could play all day without asking for money to go on this or that ride. It wasn't until the children had left home that that they had had their first and only holiday abroad in Ostend on the Belgium coast.

Sid recalled the excitement of getting a passport and sailing out of Dover and seeing the White Cliffs gradually fade into the distance and then being violently sea sick long before they docked in Ostend. He sat back in his armchair and smiled ruefully as he thought about the incident on the beach in Belgium

He had been sitting in his deck chair smoking a home rolled cigarette and thinking how much cheaper tobacco was here than back home, while his wife had been deeply engrossed in one of those romantic novels she was always reading. The afternoon had been warm and she had asked him if he would get her a drink. A little apprehensive at the thought of going off on his own in a foreign country with no grasp of the language to make any sort of purchase he did as he was bid.

Walking across the warm sands and mounting the steps up to the raised promenade which flanked the beach he had proceeded along the promenade towards the brightly coloured kiosks, which he had noticed as they had walked down from the hotel that morning. Sid scanned the beach where his eyes alighted on a woman who was stretched out topless on a bright red towel. This was a new experience for Sid, who knew that that sort of thing went on in the South of France. But for someone more use to the sands at Blackpool this was, well, different.

Bugger me he thought, I didn't know they did this in Belgium. The vision of this woman was running through Sid's mind as he selected a can of Fanta from the chiller cabinet and then fumbled around his bum bag for the correct amount of Francs as identified by the price on the tin. Pleased with his transaction in foreign currency, although not a word had been exchanged between himself and the kiosk owner, just a cursory nod between them, he began his journey back.

It was at this point that he made the fateful decision to walk back to his wife via the beach and not the esplanade. So descending the steps he walked across the beach with the warm sands passing between his toes. The route Sid had chosen was specifically designed to take him a lot closer to the now sleeping topless woman. As he approached Sid's eyes became transfixed on her bronzed form and then all of a sudden, he felt himself tumbling and the next thing he knew he was in a heap at the bottom of what felt like a moon crater.

Looking up into the sun he saw two small children peering down at him talking very quickly and incoherently to his English ear.

Sid had fallen into the sandpit that the sunbathers children had been excavating all morning.

He scrambled to his feet and picking up his cap and a slightly battered can of orange he tried to make his climb out of the sand pit as nonchalant as possible but he was conscious as made his way across the beach that everyone was looking at him and making comments to one another as to why he had fallen into the hole. Fortunately for Sid his wife had been so immersed in her book that she had been oblivious to what had befallen Sid but wanted to know why he had selected such a battered tin for her.

Happy days thought Sid as he found his eyes becoming heavy.

The next thing Sid knew was his telephone ringing. It had disturbed him from a very sound catnap and he found himself answering it not fully conscious of his actions as one does sometimes waking from a deep sleep.

'Good evening Mr Saines' said the voice at the other end 'I am calling on behalf of Mr. O'Sullivan your conservative candidate for the District Council elections. We are just checking that we can count on your vote at the forthcoming election.'

Sid was still trying to get his head into gear to understand precisely what was being said to him.

'You say you're the Tory candidate for the local election?'

'No, not quite sir, I am one of the members of Mr O'Sullivans campaign team.'

Campaign Team thought Sid, telephoning me to see if I will vote for them.

'Why can't you or he come knocking on my door like any normal politician?'

'Well if you want to discuss a particular aspect of Mr O'Sullivan's policies then I am sure either he, or someone else in his team, would be only too pleased to personally call on you Mr. err Saines.'

Sid's working class background, linked with the past experience of a Conservative Council he had had dealings with and his opinions of Maggie Thatcher all combined to give him an instant dislike of the party and what he believed the party stood for.

'You want to know 'said Sid now fully awake and in command of his faculties, 'if your bloke can count on my vote. Well tell him from me there's more chance of getting shit from a wooden horse.'

At that he slammed the receiver down. Bloody cheek he thought, we don't see the buggers from one year's end to the next and when it comes to the time they need your vote they don't even bother to send one of their lackeys round the street but get them to telephone you in the same way I am pestered by double glazing salesmen. Still you can't believe what any of them tell you.

Sid decided it was time for bed and Fluff had already determined that and had curled up on the settee determined that he wasn't going out that night. Sid opened his front door and put out the milk bottles. The light through the front door illuminated part of Sid's front garden highlighting the collection of waste that had already started to accumulate there.

'It's ok Fluff' said Sid as he closed the front door and with it leaving behind the icy blast of the wind as it whistled up his passageway and that of his next-door neighbours rattling their dustbin lids, you don't have to go out tonight.

Bloody good job thought Fluff.

Chapter 12

N ext morning Sid was sitting in the Cosy Cafe just off the High Street with a cup of strong Nescafe in front of him and an empty chair awaiting the arrival of his old ex-work mate Arthur Cooper. As he waited Sid looked around the cafe at the neatly laid out tables and walls lined with photographs and general paraphernalia associated with agriculture. Great lengths of horse brasses hung down from brightly coloured picture rails that circled the room. Interspersed with these were photographs of prize winning heifers and bulls and rosettes of various colours and sizes. Across one wall was an enlarged photograph of a countryside landscape with rolling hills and a cathedral spire in the background. Sid thought it might be Salisbury but on the other hand it could have been Hereford, he wasn't very good on his knowledge of Britain. In fact Sid had to accept that his knowledge of a lot of things was sadly lacking. He had left school at 14 and gone to work on the local farm eventually ending up as a milk delivery boy. This lack of education had left Sid often feeling inferior and so it was with so much pleasure that he had seen both his son and daughter obtain university degrees.

For his part Sid was partially dyslectic, which on occasions had been the cause of his misunderstanding a letter or the instructions of a form and so bringing him into conflict, unnecessarily, with authority. Usually the local council. This partial dyslexia had most embarrassingly manifested itself one Christmas at the garage where he had worked with Arthur. He had written a number of greeting cards for various workmates, as was the custom, and handed them out to the various recipients one tea break. He had also written one for the office secretary and left it on her desk. However, as luck would have it, she had been on holiday that day. Sid had been passing the secretary's office door later that day when he heard the sound of laughter coming from within. He instantly recognised it as emanating from Derek his boss who had been looking on his secretary's desk for some papers he had mislaid.

Sid put his head around the door and was confronted by a man convulsed in laughter with tears streaming down his cheeks.

'Here, come and look at this' he said, still giggling, 'look at what somebody has written on the front of a Christmas Card for Trudy.'

Sid looked at it and immediately realised it was his card that was causing all the merriment. For a moment Sid couldn't see why a simple white envelope with a single word on the front was causing so much merriment.

'I'm sure 'TURDY' will be pleased with her card.'

Oh shit thought Sid have I really written that, oh bugger. He had felt himself visibly colour with embarrassment.

He waited for his boss to leave the room, still chuckling to himself, and then removed the card placing it in his overalls pocket and then made a rapid exit.

Later that afternoon he had again been in the vicinity of the office when he heard the boss talking to the workshop foreman saying that the cards not here any more, the writer must have realised his mistake. To this day Sid could still hear the combined laughter of his old boss and foreman echoing in his mind.

The door of the cafe opened and in walked a small balding man wearing a winter's coat at least two sizes too large for him and a brown trilby hat a size too small such that it moved up and down as he walked towards Sid.

'Morning Cooper'

'Morning. Your turn this week I believe Sid' replied the man who obviously patronised Charity Shops.

'Yes, suppose so' he replied grudgingly, 'Usual is it?'

'Yes please Sid.'

Sid walked slowly up to the neat counter with the words Cosy Cafe picked out in what Sid thought were pieces of baked dough that had been clear varnished over.

A large glass cabinet on the counter contained a selection of cakes and scones with a gleaming stainless steel boiler and espresso coffee machine dominating the area immediately behind the counter. There was a "Cat Rescue" collection box on the counter and by the number of moggies that were sitting on the chairs in the warm cafe Sid reckoned that this must be one of the overflow centres.

Sid ordered two milky Nescafe coffees. He couldn't be doing with the frothy espresso stuff and nor could Cooper, who was never referred to as Arthur on account that there had been another Arthur in the garage where they had both worked, and so to avoid confusion Cooper had always been referred to by his surname.

Sid returned to his seat and told his pal the news of the past couple of weeks. They had not met last week owing to Arthur being away visiting his daughter somewhere in Kent, Ramsgate thought Sid.

He then recounted all of the events that he could but being careful not to break the confidentiality he had agreed with the doctor on his marital relationships and that of Ethel Treacher with the paedophile. Arthur sat and listened and when he thought it necessary he punctuated the conversation with the words 'bastards' when Sid mentioned the council and words of sympathy when he related the tale of his zipper.

For his part Cooper had little to add to the conversation this week apart from confirming he had had a pleasant time in Skegness. Well thought Sid I knew it was by the coast. Cooper said he had spent much of the time just walking around in the wind and rain as his daughter and son-in-law had both been out at work throughout the week he was with them and had been bored sitting at home on his own.

'Thought they would have had a bit of time off what with them inviting you up there 'said Sid.

'Well they both have busy jobs and I had told them not to put themselves out.'

They certainly didn't do that thought Sid to himself.

The conversation, as it often did, then turned to the past as they both recalled events and friends from the old days at the garage.

'Seen anything of 'Turbo' recently?' asked Arthur.

Turbo was the name they had given to Nobby Clark who was one of the mechanics in the workshop. The name Turbo did not describe his speed of activity, quite the contrary. The length of time he could spend carrying out a simple service on a Ford Cortina was remarkable, but he was thorough and whilst some customers would baulk at their bill for any work done on an hourly rate by Nobby they also knew that they were getting a professional and thorough job.

'No' replied Sid, 'he has been having a bit of trouble with his legs, almost housebound now I believe and can't get around much or at any pace.

'Not much change there then' said Arthur laughing at his own joke.

The staff weren't the only funny characters at the garage prompted Sid.

'Do you remember Cooper that on Sundays, to earn a bit of extra cash, we use to take it in turns to work on the petrol pumps.'

In those distant days self service at filling stations in England was in its infancy and so people had to queue to wait to be served by a petrol pump attendant.

In Sid's minds eye he could see the layout of the garage forecourt as clearly as if he was sitting looking at it instead of a picture of Constables Haywain hanging crookedly on the cafe wall.

The petrol filling station aspect of the garage complex had consisted of four pumps issuing two, three and four star petrol plus a diesel pump. There had been a sale's kiosk built into the side of the car showrooms and an air pump alongside. The pumps had been divided into two separate islands with the two and four star on one and three star and diesel on the other. Between these stood a rack containing pints and quart cans of Esso and Duckhams motor oil.

Sid related that on one Sunday afternoon the forecourt had been particularly busy and he had attended to a woman driver who had asked if he could check her oil for her. Lifting up the bonnet and from the dipstick, he had assessed that she was low on oil and possibly needed about a quart to top it up with.

Fortunately, there had been a label on the filler cap saying always use Duckhams so he was able to direct her to the Oil stand and handed her a tin of 20/50. '

'Can you put it in yourself?' he'd asked the woman. 'I'm a bit busy at the moment with other customers.'

'Err, sure' she had replied.

Whilst carrying on serving those customers waiting on the forecourt Sid became aware that the lady was still bending over the engine of her car long after she should have finished the simple job of pouring the oil into the engine.

So, as soon as he had the opportunity, he approached the car only to see a pool of oil coming from under the vehicle. Concerned as to what the woman had been doing he peered over her shoulder to see that she was attempting, and failing badly, to direct the flow of green liquid into the hole vacated by the dipstick!

The pair of friends both laughed at this as Arthur reminded Sid of a similar event. He had advised another customer that they needed more oil and that they could take it from the rack alongside the pumps. They could then come to his kiosk and pay him for however many pints they needed, of which he estimated should be a couple or maybe three at most. To his astonishment, Cooper recalled, that when he returned to the car after serving other customers he saw six empty cans alongside the vehicle.

The owner was, it turned out, trying to top up the oil, as they had been advised, by waiting to see it appear at the filler cap in the same way as he did when topping up the windscreen washer reservoir.

Not to be outdone on stories of the naivety of their past customers, Sid related the story of the driver who had come into the garage for six gallons of 3 Star, known as Shell Economy in those days. Unfortunately there was no fuel available at that grade as they were awaiting delivery from the refinery. But, to be helpful, Sid had suggested the customer put in three gallon's of 2 Star and 3 gallons of 4 Star (premium) and that this would work out the same in price etc.

'Oh' responded the motorist, 'that sounds a great idea.'

The fuel was duly put into the car and paid for but as the customer was about to walk out of the kiosk he turned to Sid and asked

'What grade will I use first, the 2 or the 4 Star?'

By this time the café had begun to fill up with people looking to have their lunch and so the two friends decided that as neither of them wanted, or were willing to buy any more cups of coffee, that they should leave.

'Same time next week Cooper'.

'Aye' he replied. 'Hopefully it will be better weather.'

They both buttoned their coats and walked out into the wet March weather looking a bit like a music-hall double act. Sid in his track suit bottoms, purple ski puffer jacket and woollen bobble hat and Arthur in his oversized coat and hat wobbling on his head as his arthritic legs took him out of the café and back to his council flat the other side of town. Sid had some shopping to do before returning home and so walked slowly along the main High Street thinking how much the old town had changed over the years.

The town clock on the Victorian town hall, now the local museum of craft and heritage, remained as a constant landmark but all around it was change. The planners he thought have completely buggered up the place, a point of view that the current local planning officers did not violently disagree with.

The building currently occupied by Superior Supermarkets, next to the town hall was testament to this. In the 1950s there had stood on the site a Victorian building which Sid had considered was proud and distinguished looking and housed the local branch of the Provincial Bank. He also thought it looked in its place with an affinity to the grandeur and size of the old town hall next to it. The building had, however, been swept aside in the desire to modernise the town centre which the then old borough council had been concerned was falling behind its neighbouring borough and could suffer economically if it did not try to compete with it.

However, the building, which replaced the old bank premises was, thought Sid, a bloody monstrosity. It had vast plate glass windows and a garish neon advertising sign. It was not the fault of the supermarket that the building was so unsympathetic. They had purchased it from the previous occupants who had left to trade from a new superstore site on the edge of town. That was another concern of Sid's and a further criticism of the lack of understanding and forethought that was the legacy of the council and its planners. Sid was not a car driver and because of this he felt disenfranchised (albeit he did not know what the word meant) insofar as he was unable to visit the out of town store due to the distance involved. He had visited it a couple of times when his son had taken him there and he had been impressed at the range of goods available, the prices, and in particular, the special offers. He, however, had to rely on the ever-dwindling town centre shops for his weekly shopping and what he considered was a second-class choice of goods at first class prices.

The old bank building was just one example, thought Sid, of the demise of his hometown's heritage. He was no architect or expert of the English townscape but even to his untrained eye he could see how the town had suffered through a lack of conservation planning and that what, in the early fifties, had been a charming cattle market town had, within 15 to 20 years, lost a great deal of its charm and character and with it the attitude of its inhabitants.

The bloody car is the biggest problem he thought. Despite from earning his living in a garage for the last 20 years of his working life, he considered that a lot of the town's problems could be related directly at the automobile.

Sid was one of the strange anomalies that whilst working in a garage he had never owned a car and never learnt to drive. This was to the great chagrin of his wife who would have loved the status of the car and the ability to get away from a town that she had never really liked, being a country girl at heart. She had been raised in one of the local villages and only moved to the town to get work on leaving school. She had met Sid at a local village dance and after they married settled down in the town because that was where the work was and it was impractical to commute daily.

Margaret never liked the town mused Sid as he tried to cross the busy High Street.

'Use the crossing you old duffer' shouted a passing motorist who had one arm on his steering wheel and the other holding a mobile phone to his ear, as he almost ran over Sid's feet. 'You want to pay more attention to what you are doing'

Sid raised a finger to the motorist and walked across the road, this time taking a little more care. He continued to reminisce about the past as he continued his journey along the High Street. The thoughts of his wife flooded back to him as he passed one of the few remaining old shops in the town, Digweeds, the wool and linen shop. His wife had always bought her wool from here. She was a good knitter and spent hours watching the television and knitting him and the kid's jumpers. A skill she had learnt from her mother who had had quite a hard time with her husband. Sid, however, had got on with him well from the day Margaret had introduced him.

His wife's father, Stan, enjoyed his drink, Truman's Brown ale in particular and it was partly due to Sid's relative distain for alcohol that attracted Margaret to him. The extent of his father-in-laws love of ale had been revealed to Sid by his wife when she one day told him of her father's great hatred for Adolf Hitler.

Initially, he had not thought that this was in any way unusual and that the vast majority of the nation probably detested the man for both what he did and what he stood for. But not Stan, he had other reasons, far more personal. One evening in the early years of WWII he had left his wife and two daughters to go drinking at the local. Whilst he was away the air raid sirens sounded and the blackout was strictly enforced. Attempting to return home in rather an intoxicated state, on a moonless night and without the benefits of street lights or the village houses to illuminate his path, he fell into a large roadside ditch where he remained unable to get out until the local milkman came by the next morning and helped him back onto the roadway.

Sid was suddenly brought back to the present day by a tap on his shoulder.

'Excuse me' said a ruddy-faced man with narrow eyes and a haircut that accentuated his almost moon shaped face. On his lapel was a large yellow rosette with the words 'Vote Matcham'.

'May I ask if you are a resident of this town sir and if so will you be voting next Thursday?'

'Yes, and maybe 'replied Sid not wishing to give much away.

'I see sir, and may I also ask if you do vote who you will be voting for?'

Sid didn't want to be kept hanging around on a street corner, as much as he usually enjoyed talking to anyone about virtually anything, but at this particular time he just wanted to complete the rest of his shopping and get home for his lunch.

'Well, if I do vote then it will be for Mr Matcham' replied Sid squinting at the name on the lapel badge.

'Well actually' replied the canvasser 'Mr Matcham is a she'.

'Oh' replied Sid who then vaguely remembered the electoral literature that had been posted through his letterbox in recent days. There was a picture of a woman amongst them but it hadn't really registered which party she represented.

'May I take your name please sir?' inquired the man, his rounded face becoming all the more beaming.

Sid duly gave him his name and address and then made off towards the Co-op to buy his lunch and a half-ounce of old Holborn with a packet of red papers.

Chapter 13

Sid arrived back at his bungalow about 12:30, pushed open the front door to find two envelopes lying on his doormat. One was a brown envelope addressed personally to Mr Sidney Saines; the other he instantly recognised as coming from the Council and addressed 'To the Occupier'.

Sid opened the letter from the District Council that he noted from the letter heading, was from the Chief Executives Department. He hadn't recalled ever receiving one from them. He read the letter with incongruous amazement and by the time he had completed it he was seething with anger. It read:-

Dear Sir/Madam

It has been brought to our attention that you have been using your council premises from which to sell merchandise for personal gain. As you are aware this is strictly against the terms and conditions of your tenancy agreement.

We would therefore respectfully request that you cease this action forthwith or we will be required to take the necessary action.

Thanking you for your cooperation.

Yours faithfully
A. Gould
Senior Assistant

Sid placed the letter down in front of him on the kitchen table.

'Bastards' he shouted as he stood staring at the piece of A4

'Absolute bastards.'

The letter could only be referring to his tomato plants for which there was a sign on his gate advising that he would be growing

"Alicante and Moneymakers this year and would his regular customers please advise him how many plant they might want this season"

Sid's great love was gardening and his pride and joy was his greenhouse from which he produced a multitude of plants, including tomatoes, all of which he grew from seed. Strangely, he disliked the taste of them but every year he received requests from friends, family and local residents for his plants that were always healthy and if properly cultivated produced good quality fruit.

To help pay for this Sid generally charged little more than the cost of the seed and compost and was happy with this arrangement as it not only provided him with an interest but also a chance to talk to his patrons and be able to afford to carry out the same service as he liked to call it year on year. Obviously, thought Sid, some vindictive individual has decided to report me to the Council.

Sid sat at his kitchen table with a cup of tea, he didn't

fancy the lunch that he had just purchased from the Co-op. He felt too annoyed and upset to think that one of his neighbours had been so small minded and vindictive as to report him for selling some tomato plants.

Seems I don't have any option he thought. However felt he had to make some kind of protest that he was being victimised. Unable to put his thoughts into writing he decided he would pay the Chief Executives department, and in particular Mr Gould, a visit that afternoon.

Sid thought the Chief Executives Department was even more plusher than the District Treasurer's. A deep red carpet was on the floor of the reception area and at a very expensive looking black desk in the centre of it sat not one but two women, one of whom, Sid thought he recognised but couldn't quite place where from.

The other female was a small blonde girl young enough to still be at school. The older of the two spoke as he approached.

'Good afternoon Sir can I help you?'

'I would like to see someone in charge about this letter' said Sid in his most authoritive manner.

The woman scanned the letter.

'Do you have an appointment?'

'No' replied Sid his voice and mannerisms beginning to alter, 'I haven't, this was an unsolicited letter and in response this is equally an unsolicited call.'

Pleased with his reply Sid waited patiently while the receptionist, who Sid now thought might previously have worked on the cooked meat counter at Budgen's, spoke quietly into the telephone.

'Mr Gould is busy at the moment 'she said as she replaced the receiver but his colleague Mr Simpkinson is coming down to see if he can help. Please take a seat he shouldn't keep you long.

Sid thanked the receptionist, thinking to himself she's come up in the world a bit and sat down to wait.

It was a full ten minutes before Alan Simkinson appeared in front of Sid.

'Mr Staines' he said 'How can I help you?'

'The names Saines' replied Sid.

'Sorry' responded the official, 'please come this way where we can have some privacy.'

He took Sid into a small side room.

'Can I get you a tea or coffee?'

Remarkably civil thought Sid 'Yes I will have a coffee please with one sugar.'

The man left the room and returned shortly with two plastic cups of vending machine brew. Not that gracious thought Sid as he sipped the dark brown chemical concoction he had been given.

'It's about this letter' said Sid placing it on the table between them.

'Ah yes, I believe that you have been selling garden plants and the like from your house.'

'I have orders for precisely 27 tomato plants at 25 pence each this year' replied Sid.

'Just so, and as such you are carrying out an operation which is contrary to your tenancy agreement.'

'Oh come on' retorted Sid,' surely that clause is designed to stop people earning a living from their Council premises not for the likes of me who only want some pin money for next year's seeds and compost.'

'It's the thin end of the wedge sir' he replied. 'If we condone what you are doing it could be used against us if we try to bring a similar action against a more blatant and lucrative financial operation.'

'I don't want to be seen as an informer' said Sid 'but what about number 37 across the road from me? He's 'ad a for sale sign on his car for the last three weeks, how does that differ'?

'It's a matter of degrees Mr Saines, we have not received any complaint about this but now you have raised it we will certainly investigate.'

'Well don't tell him it was me who told you' responded Sid, 'he's a big bugger'!

'Now returning to your case Mr Saines I'm afraid you must remove your sign and stop trading. That's the bottom line. If you continue we will have to consider your tenancy agreement!'

'Okay' replied Sid I have got the message, just a bunch of little killjoys you are up here, but I would love to know who it was that reported me.'

'Oh I can tell you that' replied Mr Simkinson, 'it was Miss Johnson our Chief Housing Officer. She noticed the sign a couple of weeks ago when she was visiting your next door neighbour, I believe.'

Sid was stunned into silence. Why the vindictive cow he thought.

'I'm sorry I can't spare any more time with you on this matter Mr Saines, I have to prepare for tomorrow's elections.'

At this point Mr Simkinson rose from the table, stretched out his hand to shake Sid's and ushered him from the room. Sid left the council offices and walked slowly home. There are rules for the rich and ones for the poor buggers like me he thought.

Chapter 14

The local elections came and went; Sid did his duty and duly voted for the Liberal Democrat candidate, as he had promised. His political convictions and prejudices had prevented him from voting for the Conservatives and he knew the Labour Party candidate to be a local second hand car dealer, a real 'wide boy' and in his opinion not suitable to be given the responsibility of a councillor spending his rates.

However, despite Sid's vote, the Lib Dems came a poor third in the ward with the Conservatives not only securing that seat but also wresting overall control of the Council away from the current Lib Dem/Labour coalition.

Don't suppose it will make a lot of difference to me he thought as he read the results posted up outside the town hall the next morning. He was, however, soon to be proved wrong.

About six weeks after the election, Sid received a letter from the Council. On opening it he noted from the heading that it was from the Chief Executives Department and formally addressed him as Mr Staines.

Apart from the letter the envelope contained some glossy leaflets and a small booklet all with the heading 'Apse Housing Association.'

Sid read the letter and its accompanying literature carefully. There were some words and phrasing which he didn't fully understand but generally it confirmed that the council were considering handing over its council housing stock to the housing association. The letter outlined the likely timetable and confirmed that part of the agreement would be that all rents would be capped for 12 months after any transfer and that for the following 5 years they would not be permitted to rise by more than the rate of inflation plus 1%. Sid was not sure what this really meant or the implications of having a private landlord. However, the literature setting out the credentials of Apse Housing Association looked impressive. They had, the brochures confirmed, already secured the contract for the adjacent Council (Wellesley District) housing stock and by all accounts the majority of the tenants were happy with the changeover. The letter confirmed that a decision on whether to take the matter further would be made at the next full council meeting to be held in 5 weeks time and that in the intervening period a public meeting and exhibition would be held to provide more information to existing tenants.

Sid attended the meeting, which was held in the town's only theatre 'The Royal' which had previously been the Regent Cinema, or local fleapit, as it had affectionately been known as. It was years since Sid had been inside it. The last time he recalled it must have been to see "Bridge over the River Kwai."

The meeting turned out to be a lively affair with most of the residents criticising the local council and wanting to know what guarantees there would be of security of tenure, rent rises and future maintenance.

Apse Housing, Sid thought, came across as a very professional organisation and whilst he was always wary of change as long as there were sufficient safeguards put in place then he believed that they probably could not be worse than the Councils current housing department.

This appeared to be the general consensus of the meeting who were promised that with the added private funds available to the Association their first task would be, if the deal with the council went through, to carry out a maintenance audit of all properties and begin a rigorous and ongoing improvement scheme. One that would include central heating for all properties within seven years, and hopefully five.

Sid liked the sound of this. I could point out all of the problems I've got in my bungalow that I have been waiting years to have 'sorted out.' Actually most of these were cosmetic as the local council maintenance team had been regular visitors to Sid's house over the years replacing washers on dripping taps, fixing leaking guttering and security locks. Regardless of this however, Sid considered he had a poor deal as a tenant of Creekleigh District Council.

He was therefore delighted to read in the local paper the following Thursday that the full council had voted for Apse Housing Association to take over their housing stock as from 1st April. He also read with even more pleasure the rest of the article which explained that as a result of the transfer of the council's housing there would be the opportunity for additional savings. This would be brought about, the paper said, through the amalgamation of certain council departments and a restructuring of its management team. The posts it revealed of Chief Planning Officer would be combined with that of the District Engineers to create a Directorate of Environmental Services and that the Chief Housing Officers post would go.

The article concluded with a comment from the outgoing Chief Housing Officer that she had enjoyed her time working for Creekleigh District Council but that she thought it was a good time to move on to newer pastures. (Very apt thought Sid as he had always considered her a cow). She also confirmed that she would not be seeking a position with the new Housing Association.

They probably didn't want her thought Sid who sat at his kitchen table with the widest of smiles upon his face. Poor Miss Johnson, perhaps I should send her a bunch of flowers or maybe some of me tomato plants.

Chapter 15

The honeymoon period between Sid and his new landlords didn't last long. Six weeks into his new tenure he received a letter, as did all the tenants of the bungalows in his block, advising of the pending visit of their surveyor to assess the future maintenance requirements of the individual housing units.

Sid had prepared a list to ensure that he didn't forget anything and was ready for the Association man when he knocked at his door on a bright sunny May morning.

'Good morning Mr Saines, I am Mike Gardener of the Apse Housing Association, I believe you have been expecting me'

'Certainly have' replied Sid as he invited him into his lounge.

Mike Gardener looked around.

'Very good decorative order sir' he exclaimed 'you obviously look after your place'.

Sid beamed with pride.

'Well I try to.'

'Do you mind if I have a look around both inside and out?'

'Please be my guest replied Sid, would you like a cup of tea?'

'No thank you he replied I have 7 other houses to look at today after this one so I must crack on.'

'I understand' replied Sid who also decided against a tea and lit his pipe instead.

Sid reckoned that the surveyor only spent about ten minutes looking around the place making notes and taking the odd measurement. When he had finished he returned to the lounge to be asked immediately by Sid what his verdict was.

'No verdict' replied the surveyor 'I have been on a fact finding mission and have made a note of all the points I need to complete my report'

'Before you go' said Sid 'I have made a list of all the defects I have found and I am sure you will have found more being a professional.'

'Thank you Mr Saines' said Mike looking at the not inconsiderable list he had been given. 'I am sure it will be very helpful to me. Thank you for your time.'

Sid smiled as he said goodbye to the man and watched him walk up the pathway of his house and off up the road into the distance.

Strange thought Sid I understood he had a number of other houses in the area to look at and that he would be visiting old mother Stepney next door after me. He won't find her house with all those cats as clean as mine he thought as he closed his door. It was some time later in the day that Sid had the telephone call from the Housing Association that was to create untold anger and misery.

About 3pm Sid's telephone rang, the female voice on the other end started the conversation by confirming that she was calling on behalf of Apse Housing Association and in particular on behalf of Mr Gardener their Surveyor. The caller went on to explain that owing to illness it would not be possible for their surveyor to visit that day and that it might be several weeks before they could rearrange the appointment as their representative had been hospitalised following a car accident a couple of days ago.

For a moment Sid was speechless and then he shouted into the receiver 'What do you mean won't be able to see me for a few weeks he came this morning.'

'I am sorry Mr Saines' replied the female voice but that is not possible.'

'Are you calling me a liar' Sid began to raise his voice, a clear sign that he was becoming angry.'

'No Sir' but I am afraid   you must have been mistaken I personally visited Mr Gardener at the general hospital last night and his leg was in plaster and in traction, there is no way he could have visited you or anyone else today.'

'Well who the hell was it then' replied Sid

'He said he worked for your lot and that his name was Mike Gardener.'

'I have to repeat sir that Mike, I mean Mr Gardener, could not have physically visited you today' said the woman who was by now becoming increasingly concerned at both the tenor of Sid's voice and the fact that he believed he had been visited earlier that day by someone who could not

116

possibly have done so.

'Well who the hell was he' shouted Sid he had a Clip board and knew that I was supposed to be visited by your organisation today.'

'I am afraid I don't know Mr Saines all I can reiterate is that he does not work for us. Did he show you his ID Card?'

Sid thought for a moment.

'No he didn't'. I didn't think the need to ask for it as I was expecting someone and he fitted the bill, seemed very professional and knew what he was there for. Are you sure he wasn't a replacement for your bloke?'

By this time Sid was beginning to become un-nerved by his conversation, a feeling that was deepened by the female voice on the other end asking

'Have you checked you belongings since the visitor left?'

At this point Sid dropped the receiver and rushed into his bedroom just avoiding the cat that was sprawled across the threshold of the door.

'Out of the way Fluff' he shouted and opened the bottom draw of his 3-draw chest. 'Ah, its still there' he sighed as he saw his large Quality Street Tin with the female on the lid staring up at him.

He then realised that the tin should be hidden beneath his underwear at the bottom of the drawer. He feverishly grabbed the tin and immediately he felt a lump in his throat, the lightness of the tin told him it was empty.

He frantically yanked the top off the tin only to see his own reflection coming back from the polished bottom of the empty container.

Sid just stood and stared at the empty vessel.

'It gone' he said to himself 'it's all bloody gone'

At this point Sid suddenly realised that he could hear a disembodied voice coming from his lounge; it was the lady from the Housing Association who had become concerned at the sudden cessation of their telephone conversation. But Sid was still too overcome by a mixture of anger and disbelief to return to the phone he simply stood in his small bedroom staring at the empty tin as tears began to well up in his eyes.

Sid continued to stare into the shinning void but eventually he responded to the ever more frantic shouts of the woman from the Housing Association.

'I've been robbed' stuttered Sid down the receiver.

'Oh my goodness' replied the caller. 'You had better call the police and meanwhile I will alert the management at this end as to what has transpired.'

Sid dropped the receiver and returned to his small bedroom with the bottom draw of his chest gaping open and the empty Quality Street tin lying on his bed. He sat on the eiderdown beside it and began to cry, something he had not done since his wife had died. Two thousand pounds in notes of various denominations had been in that tin. It had been part of his savings that he did not want to declare to the Council so as to ensure that he would not fall foul of the maximum savings allowance that would have prevented him from securing housing benefit and rate rebate. The money had been hard earned, all the gardening work money had gone straight into the receptacle as had other windfall money like the odd £10 win on the lottery and the government's one off winter fuel allowance.

Now the money was no more, the bastard bogus surveyor had done a runner with it.

Sid felt annoyed with himself for letting the man have the freedom of his house, something he was normally very careful not to do to strangers.

After a while Sid's self pity began to turn to anger as he thought the longer I leave letting the authorities know the more time the thieving bastard will have to get away.

Sid blew his nose on his usual Andrex tissue and wiped his reddened eyes and walked slowly to the telephone and for only the second time in his life dialled 999, the first time being when he had set fire to his chimney and had to call out the local fire brigade.

On being asked by the Emergency Operator which service he required Sid asked for the Police and was politely asked if it was an emergency.

'Yes it bloody well is he replied I have been robbed and the longer the police take to get here and obtain the information the further away the bastard who nicked my money will be.'

The operator politely, but firmly, advised Sid that his request did not constitute an emergency and was given the number of his local police station.

'Can't you put me though?' he enquired.

He was again told that he would have to make the contact and with that the operator cut short the conversation.

Sid duly telephoned his local station and briefly outlined the recent events. He was advised that an officer would be with him as soon as possible but regretted that it might not be right away as they were short staffed with officers being deployed in the county town on security duty for the visit of the deputy prime minister.

Bloody right ain't it, thought Sid, beginning to regain his composure and his old feistiness. Hundreds of police to look after one bloody big bloke who looks as if he can look after himself whereas me, a poor old pensioner, has to wait until he is safely belted up in his Jag and back on his way to London.

However, around two hours later a police patrol car pulled up outside Sid's bungalow and an officer stepped out. Sid reckoned he was in his thirties a tall man with short regulation hair and his peaked cap tucked underneath his arm.

Sid opened the front door of his house and before the officer could utter a word he demanded to see his warrant card. This was duly produced by PC Winterbourne and was studied hard by Sid who looked at the photograph and then at the Officer.

'Not very flattering is it sir' said the constable trying to add a degree of informality to the visit.

'The camera certainly wasn't very kind to you son' responded Sid, 'that hat makes your ears look big.'

Constable Winterbourne cleared his throat and asked Sid if he was happy with his credentials. Sid nodded and invited him into his lounge. As he sat down on the well worn settee alongside the cat Sid enquired if he wanted a cup of tea but the officer declined saying that this was his last call of the day and that he would be off duty soon and home to his dinner.

'Now then, Mr Saines isn't it?'

'Yes.'

'I understand that you were robbed today by a man claiming to work for the new housing association.'

'That's right. The bugger conned his way into my house and stole all me savings from right under me very nose.'

PC Winterbourne began to write in his notebook as Sid related the events of the afternoon.

Stopping him only to clarify various points the constable listened intently and when Sid had completed his narrative he looked at him and said how sorry he was that this had happened but could not understand how he had been so off his guard as to let the man have a free rein of his house.

Sid admitted that it was out of character and that he had been so disarmed by the man and the fact that he had actually been expecting someone from the housing association that he had been duped.

The officer enquired if any thing else had been stolen but Sid could not answer as he had not checked the remainder of his premises as he had been too preoccupied with the loss of the money.

PC Winterbourne said that he would contact HQ from his car and that it was likely he would have a visit from a member of their laboratory staff who would take fingerprint details from the tin.

'Do you recall if the man wore gloves' asked the constable.

'No, I am sure he didn't' replied Sid 'cos I remember seeing a very large ring on his left hand'

'Ah' replied the policeman, getting out his notebook again, you haven't told me about this.

'Yes' replied Sid 'now I come to think of it it was a large gold ring, having the letter J or T on it.'

'Anything else you can remember about the man's description' asked the constable.

'No nothing more than I have already told you' replied Sid.

'OK Mr Saines thank you for your help and as I have said someone will be in contact'

As Sid showed him to the door he asked 'What happens next'

'Well', I will make my report and we will run it through the computer to see if there are any similarities between this and any other recent crimes. I would think that this type of crime is unlikely to be a one off and that the perpetrator is likely to have offended and will strike again.'

'What chances do you think of me getting me money back' enquired Sid.

'I have to advise you Mr Saines that cash in low denomination notes must be one of the easiest of items to dispose of and therefore I have to tell you that the chances are slim, but we will of course try to do all we can.'

Sid thanked the constable for his time and understanding as he stood up to leave but found that this was hampered by the presence of Sid's old tomcat that had stretched out alongside him and was now resting its head against his leg.

'Sorry puss' said the constable 'I have to leave and disturb you.'

'Don't worry about him' replied Sid 'it's about time he moved, 'bin there virtually all day he has, his bladder must be bursting.'

The officer smiled, 'What's his name sir, I am a bit of a cat fancier'

'He's called Fluff.'

Not very imaginative thought PC Winterbourne as he stroked Fluff on the head and then bade farewell to Sid. Sid returned to his lounge and immediately began to check if anything else was missing. He was pretty sure the money was the only missing item and could not imagine what else could have been worth stealing that the thief could have inconspicuously concealed on his person. Sid was wrong for as he checked through the drawers of his dressing table he found that the old jewellery box belonging to his late wife had been disturbed and that missing from it was both the engagement and wedding ring.

Sid felt sick as the water formed in his eyes causing him to blink through his blurred vision into the open box.

He felt defiled as well as annoyed and upset that these precious items had been taken from him. They were not worth a great deal as at the time he bought them he didn't have much money to spend but in terms of sentimental value they were priceless.

Got to pull myself together thought Sid, better go up to the cop shop and advise them of these additional bits and pieces that have disappeared.

As Sid left his home he was more careful than ever about locking the premises. Bit like locking the stable door after the horse had bolted he thought but lightening can strike twice. He walked slower than usual into the town engrossed in his thoughts that constantly saw the image of the robber flash across his mind.

'Bastard' he kept muttering underneath his breath to the

extent that two old ladies he passed, who were sitting on the bench outside the cemetery stopped their animated conversation to stare at Sid and tutted before continuing their character assassination of a mutual friend.

Sid arrived outside the local police station, a building he was thankful not to be too familiar with, and entered through the heavily varnished dark portal. A plate on the door announced that the station was closed each evening and that for assistance after 6pm the number below should be called.

Bloody marvellous ain't it thought Sid. Less Bobbies on the beat, and now there are not even any at the local nick after teatime. The criminals in this country must think its Christmas every day.

As Sid entered the station he was confronted by a large poster stating ' Lock it or Loose it" pinned to the wall and next to it was a reception desk not unlike the one in the Council offices Housing Department but with a burly uniformed policeman with sergeants stripes on his sleeve standing behind it.

As Sid approached the officer was engrossed with a telephone conversation. He stood and waited, and listened to the conversation as best he could, given that he could only hear half of the discussion.

The conversation was clearly about stolen property thought Sid and the sergeant was talking to the person from whom the goods had been removed.

In front of the policeman on the counter was a brown paper bag and protruding from it was the end of a baseball bat. Strange thought Sid who continued to eavesdrop on the conversation.

'Yes sir' replied the sergeant' we have a juvenile being held at the station at this very moment who is helping us with our enquiries into a number of local burglaries.' The officer stopped explaining and began nodding and occasionally saying 'yes and no' into the receiver.

'Yes sir we are trying to connect him with the robbery of your premises last week. Could you confirm if one of the items taken was an American baseball bat' asked the sergeant as he casually fingered the narrow end of the wooden implement in front of him.

'You can confirm that one has gone missing, thank you sir.'

Again there was a pause before he responded with 'why do I ask about the baseball bat as it wasn't on your list of items taken. Well sir the juvenile when apprehended has admitted to a number of other burglaries and remembers taking the said bat from your house.'

'No sir, we have not recovered any other items as yet.'

'Where did we find the baseball bat?'

'In the Coop window sir, the youth used it to break the plate glass window but left it behind in his haste to escape'

The conversation concluded with the sergeant requesting the person on the other end of the line to come to the police station in the near future in order to positively identify the bat and reclaim it.

Replacing the receiver Sergeant Adams, as the sign 'Today's Duty Officer' behind him identified, turned to Sid and apologized for keeping him waiting and asked if he could be of assistance.

Sid briefly outlined the story of the day as the sergeant

genially nodded and occasionally expressed his sympathy. He then took a note of the description of the two rings but Sid was never very good at describing these types of articles and so what the sergeant got was that they were both round and gold. The engagement ring had a small blue diamond set in it and the wedding ring was distinctive insofar as it had 'With Love Sid' engraved inside it.

The sergeant promised he would pass the information onto PC Winterbourne when he came on duty the next morning.

'Any leads yet?' asked Sid.

'No, sorry sir' replied the officer, 'we have circulated your description of the man and the Housing Association are also very concerned that this man could strike again under the pretence of being one of their employees.'

'Shouldn't people be warned about him' said Sid. 'Why haven't the local radio station given out some kind of alert.'

'I believe that the Association have considered this matter Mr.Saines but I understand that they think that this might just be a one off and they didn't want to unduly worry the older tenants in particular.'

'It will worry them a darned sight more if the bugger strikes again' said Sid. 'Some old dear, not as strong as me, could 'ave a heart attack or something if they have 'appen to them what 'append to me.'

'Well, may I suggest you take it up directly with the Association Mr Saines. I am sure they would be interested in hearing from you again.'

I might just do that thought Sid as he bode goodbye to the sergeant and walked out onto Church Street.

Sid contemplated visiting the new offices of the Housing Association but suddenly felt hungry and realised that in his concern for his stolen property he had not eaten for a considerable time. He consequently decided to call into the local Co-op supermarket to get some cheese and a fresh loaf of bread with the intent of making himself a welsh rarebit on his return home.

On reaching the shop he was reminded of his visit to the police station by the large sheet of plywood that covered one of the plate glass windows of the frontage. Once inside the store Sid could see the extent of the damage to the window still awaiting replacement.

He must have been a big lad to do that amount of damage to the glass thought Sid. He certainly gave it a hefty thwack with that baseball bat.

Sid duly bought his half a pound of cheddar (he refused to buy anything in metric weights) that was on special offer and his large white family loaf. (He didn't like wholemeal and the grains from a granary loaf got beneath his ill fitting top set of dentures.)

Chapter 16

On arriving home Sid had just completed the melting of his cheese onto the bread under his gas grill when the telephone rang.

Bugger thought Sid, who's that at this time of day interrupting me preparing me grub.

Sid lifted the receiver to find that it was the deputy chief executive of the housing association calling to ask after his welfare and if it would be convenient for one of his officers' to call and see him that afternoon.

'Certainly' replied Sid, anxious to get back to his cheese on toast, 'But make sure he brings some identification with him.'

The caller chuckled 'Certainly Mr Saines'

'I ain't laughing' replied Sid.

'No, sorry' responded the deputy suddenly realizing his insensitivity. 'Would 3 pm be okay?'

'That will be fine' said Sid 'Who will it be so that I know who to expect.'

'Mr. Mathias' replied the caller 'and thank you.'

As Sid replaced the handset he could smell his cheddar burning in the kitchen and on withdrawing the grill pan he was confronted with a blackened mess that was immediately dispatched into the waste bin with an expletive.

As 3 o'clock came round Sid opened the front door of his bungalow to Mr. Mathias. He was a man of West Indian extraction with a baldhead, flashing white teeth and immaculately dressed in a well-fitted dark grey suit.

The visitor handed over his identity card without being asked by Sid who studied it carefully before admitting Mr. Mathias into his home.

The representative of the Housing Association formally introduced himself and said

'I have come to apologise formally on behalf of the Association for any distress that has been caused.'

'It was not your fault I was robbed Sid explained. 'It's just that the bastard that robbed me used your association as a means of gaining entry to my house along with my misguided trust. How the hell he happened to know I was expecting someone from your place I don't know'

'Well, that's what I have in part come to explain Mr Saines. I thought it should come from us rather than the police.'

'As you know a Mr. Gardener was due to come and survey your property but that due to a road accident he ended up in hospital and so could not fulfil his appointment with you.'

'Yeah' replied Sid 'the woman at your office who telephoned me after I had been robbed told me all about that'

'Well' continued Mr Mathias 'As a result of his accident a number of his papers went missing including his itinerary for the day you were robbed. These obviously got into the hands of the man who you thought was one of our employees and unfortunately you were his selected victim.'

'Due to the loss of these papers and, to be honest the state of the filing system we inherited from the old council housing department, I am afraid that we were too late in advising you of the situation.'

Too bloody right thought Sid and still the council are causing me problems!

'Now of course we have told the local CID about the situation and they are carrying out further investigations both into your robbery and the details surrounding Mr. Gardener's accident.

'Well that's all well and good ' responded Sid 'but that still means I have lost a lot of money and now it seems that your organization, through their negligence, are partly responsible'

At this point Sid began to feel that he might now be able to turn something to his advantage.

'Although I have come around to see you personally to apologise on behalf of the Association for any distress the robbery has caused you we cannot admit any liability responded the visitor.'

'Distress' shouted Sid, raising his voice in annoyance and the condescending way he thought he was being talked to. 'Seems to me I have a good case in trying to sue your lot for negligence'

'I would strongly advise against that Mr Saines' replied his visitor also changing his tone.

'And why is that' inquired Sid staring directly into his visitors eyes.

'Well, as a result of your recent misfortune we have naturally inspected your files which we inherited from the District Council.'

'So' responded Sid, 'I aint got nothing to hide, all my rent is paid up to date and on time.'

It certainly is Mr Saines but we have noted from your file you have been claiming Housing Benefit allowance and rate rebate based on your earnings and savings.'

'Correct,' replied Sid very indignantly. 'The Council had evidence of all my income from me pension and the savings in my West Shires Building Society account and as a result I was told I was entitled to those allowances.'

'Very true' came the response 'But the savings you declared to the council were not the sum total of your money were they Mr. Saines? You had other savings that you did not declare!'

Sid sat in his armchair stunned.

Eventually he stuttered 'You mean that you are saying I ain't entitled to some of the benefits I've been claiming.'

'Correct' came the curt response. 'We of course do not know how long you had the money prior to its removal by the thief but clearly it was for some time which could make you liable to have to pay back part of the rebate you have been claiming.'

'You bastard' shouted Sid unable to control his emotions. 'You come round here under the pretext of offering me sympathy only to suddenly spring this one on me. I had hoped you would be better than the old Council. Seems to me that you are the same but in a different guise.'

'I am sorry you feel that way Mr Saines because the main point of my visit was to say that given our involvement, albeit unwillingly, in your financial loss the Association were in this instance willing to come to an agreement with you insofar as for your part you do not involve us in any adverse publicity or seek legal claims and for our part we will ensure that the financial regulations involving your claims are, lets say, forgotten.'

Again Sid sat stunned for the moment. Just what were the implications of what he was being told? Sid was not so naïve as to realise that he did not have the wherewithal to fight the Association and that whilst he knew that he could make things very uncomfortable for them for a while he was likely to be the ultimate looser.

'Okay' he eventually responded 'Seems I have no option but I ain't paying any more rent.'

'No, of course not Mr Saines, you no longer have any additional undisclosed savings do you?'

'No I ain't' replied Sid emphatically 'Some other bastard has got that.'

'Well then replied Mr Mathias it seems that our records now correspond with your situation.'

At that point Sid's visitor rose from his armchair opposite Sid to leave. He stretched out his hand to shake his tenants who reluctantly responded.

'I hope our conversation has been of benefit to you Mr Saines and that you and your savings are soon reunited.'

I bet you do, thought Sid, just so you can get your hands on some of me hard earned rebate.

The truth was however that neither of them was to see the money that had long since left the district and all enquiries by the local police were to prove fruitless

Chapter 17

Sid sat down and opened the brown envelope that had arrived at the same time as his letter from the council but had been overlooked due to the contents of the official communication. Sid had placed it behind the clock and had totally forgotten it until he had chanced to move it to do a bit of dusting.

He pulled out the contents to reveal that years holiday brochure from the local travel company he had used for the last 5 or 6 years. Lancaster Holidays were a coach hire company operated and run as a small family business by Bill and Bob Lancaster   They had, a few years ago found a small niche market for themselves in arranging short holidays to destinations throughout the country for generally the older holidaymaker. They were able to make local collections and what appealed to Sid and a number of the other regular customers of Lancaster's was that once on their coach they were able to settle down for the whole journey.

Sid hated the feeder coach system operated by some of the National Coach companies where they converged on a Motorway Service Centre and everyone swapped coaches to destinations throughout the nation. The personal service offered by Bob and Bill ensured repeat bookings every year and as such a good relationship had grown up between them and their passengers.

Every year they would organise six or seven holidays, all hotel based, which would act as a centre for the week, or ten days maximum, activity.

Sid immediately started to look through the brochure which was not a glossy production but one that had been prepared "In House" using a desk top publishing package. Sid did not care about this, his main concern was where they were going this year and how much.

From the index at the front Sid noted that this year they had the option of 7 destinations, which included Llandudno, Scarborough, Southport, Scotland, Bournemouth, Isle of Wight and Devon. Just the regular places again thought Sid. Don't want to go to Llandudno again this year and I've been to Scarborough twice and both times it just pissed down with rain the whole week. When are they going to Bournemouth? I like it there they have some damned good shows on at the pier and that new conference centre on the sea front.

Sid noted that they were scheduled to stay a week at the St Swithin's Hotel (sounds like it should be in Scarborough thought Sid) at the end of June. The price per room, including all travel and a number of daily excursions was £395 plus a single room supplement of £5 per night. This extra £35 on his bill really annoyed Sid who one year had tried to get old Mrs Morgan to share a room with him (single beds of course) but she had refused point blank and hadn't spoken to him since that day.

The excursions were something that Sid also enjoyed, particularly as he was on his own. It helped pass the time in company, which he generally knew and enjoyed.

He often only met up with other travellers once a year on these trips. As the clients of the holiday company came from the surrounding local towns and villages and so were not local to one another they were unable to continue the relationships once the coach returned.

That's it thought Sid, its Bournemouth for me this year.

With this decision made Sid, completed the attached reservation form and made a note for himself to visit the building society to get a cheque made out for the deposit. Sid did not have a chequebook and so relied on the services of the West Shires Building Society to write a cheque on the rare occasions when he needed one.

The day of the holiday dawned with the weather far from conducive to a seaside vacation. The sky was a threatening shade of grey and the wind was blowing the rubbish around Sid's front garden as he frantically raced around trying to collect it before he departed for the coast. He had had his old battered suitcase ready and packed for over an hour when the coach pulled up outside of his bungalow. He immediately recognised a couple of regulars, Sybil and Eric, looking out of the window and waving at him. The house was locked-up; Fluff was to be looked after by one of the neighbours, he had given his son and daughter an address in case of emergencies. Sid was off to Bournemouth and, he hoped, the sun.

The journey south was relatively uneventful with the various occupants getting to know one another whilst the regulars caught up with the news of what a particular individual had been doing since they last met.

In the case of some it was 3 or 4 years since their

individual holidays had coincided.

The stop on the motorway services caused Sid some consternation, as he could not believe how much they were charging in the cafeteria for a pot of tea. He had however devised his own way of getting his moneys worth of tea.

Sid would buy a pot of tea for one and ensure that he took plenty of cartons of milk and packets of sugar from the display counter. He would then consume the tea and return to the counter complaining that it was too strong and ask if he could have some extra hot water.

This ploy he found was generally accepted and so with the refilled pot of boiling water he would return to his seat and from his pocket retrieve a fresh tea bag brought from home. This way Sid had 3 or 4 cups of tea for the price of one. A fair deal he thought given the extortionate price he was being charged.

The Hotel St Swithin's was a small two-storey establishment, set about 10 minutes walk from the sea front. Sid's room was small but comfortable with a double bed and en-suite facilities. The view from his room was uninspiring with the rear of another hotel dominating his vision. He was however just able to glimpse the sea between it and another long low building of indeterminate function. It was to turn out to be a nightclub!

Sid gauged the quality of a hotel by two main factors, the size of the food portions at dinner, and the comfort of the bed.

In terms of the former he was to find out that evening that he was unlikely to go hungry that week but the beds were too soft and Sid had great difficulty in sleeping. The problem however was further exacerbated by the noise, which that night, emanated from the Club.

After a very satisfying dinner Sid returned to his room feeling weary after the day's travelling and decided to have an early night with a view to having an early morning walk on the beach before breakfast. However, soon after slipping into a gentle sleep Sid was awoken by a continuous repetitive dull thud that reverberated around his room.

At first Sid could not focus his mind on precisely where he was, but as he sat up in bed and looked around the unfamiliar surroundings he realised that he wasn't at home in Creekleigh but in a hotel room that he thought was throbbing. His attention was then drawn towards his open window through which he now determined was coming the sound that had disturbed his sleep. He had been dreaming that he was being chased by The Tiller Girls, a dance troupe that he had especially enjoyed when watching Sunday Night at the London Palladium on TV many years ago. After closing the window and burying his head under his pillow Sid eventually got back to a fitful sleep but was unable to return to his earlier dream.

The receptionist was sitting on her stool wistfully thinking that she should be sunning herself on a Greek Island instead of looking after the bookings at a hotel for geriatrics when she glanced up from her copy of Hello Magazine to see Sid Saines standing before her.

He was wearing the typical British holidaymakers' uniform of pale slacks, a bright open necked polo shirt, and a peaked cap with the word Ferrari emblazoned on it, dark socks and opened toed sandals.

'I wish to complain' was Sid's opening address to the receptionist.

'Certainly sir and what appear to be the trouble. Are you not satisfied with your room?'

'No I am not. I didn't get a wink of sleep last night due to that thunderous racket coming from that bloody nightclub next door. There was nothing in your brochure that said that I would have wall-to-wall booming all night. It would have been enough to disturb me fillings if I hadn't got false teeth.'

The receptionist smiled at this point as in his haste that morning to go down to the hotel lobby and complain Sid had forgotten to extract his teeth from the glass in the bathroom and therefore as he spoke, or rather shouted, she had the unnerving glimpses of his nicotine ravaged gums flashing at her.

'I am very sorry your sleep was disturbed sir' replied the receptionist with her eyes still drawn inexplicably to Sid's mouth. 'What is your room number?'

'Lucky 7' retorted Sid 'The one out the back with no view but an unrestricted noise corridor to the music from hell.'

She looked down her register. 'Ah yes Mr Stains.'

'No, not Stains, Saines' shouted Sid becoming even more irritable.

'Ah yes, sorry about that must have been a slip of the word processor. You must appreciate Mr Saines that this is a town centre site and therefore the presence of night entertainment is a natural consequence that has to be accepted for the convenience of the hotel's location.'

'To a degree I accept that' replied Sid. 'But there is a limit to the noise and disturbance one should be expected to put up with especially at 2 o'clock in the morning.'

Carol, the receptionist agreed that it wasn't an ideal situation.

'As we are not fully booked Mr Saines I can offer you alternative accommodation in our west wing at the side of the hotel but I am afraid that unlike your current room I does not have a sea view.'

'Sea view' exclaimed Sid. 'You need to be a bloody contortionist to see the briny from my window, just so long as it's away from the bloody boom of that disco I will take it.'

At that the receptionist slowly got up from her stool took the keys off the rack on the wall and asked Sid to follower her. The room was on the first floor of the hotel and overlooked a small garden which, whilst not the sea, was acceptable to Sid.

'Will this be acceptable?' quizzed Carol.

'I think this will do just fine' replied Sid looking round the room and finding it almost a mirror image of the one with its own sound system.

That evening after returning from an excursion to Poole Pottery with the rest of his fellow travellers Sid felt unusually tired and so after dinner he gave his apologise to some of his cohorts and said he was going to have an early night.

'Good idea' said Sybil. 'You had a rough night last night what with that disco and all, you get some shut eye coz were out again tomorrow to Swanage and it's an early start.'

'Night all, see you at breakfast.'

Sid was soon asleep, tucked up in bed happy in the

knowledge that the disco was on the other side of the hotel and that its sounds would not interfere with his sleep any more. However, he was suddenly awakened by a deep rumbling sound that grew louder until it broke in a crescendo of clattering. There then followed a general hubbub of raised voices to again be followed by a deep rumbling and what sounded like a violent crash of he knew not what.

'What the hell is that' shouted Sid to an empty room.

After two more episodes of rumbling and crashing Sid got up and hurriedly put some clothes on over his pyjamas and went downstairs.

Once in the lobby Sid found that the reception area had closed for the evening and so he headed for the only other area that he knew might be open at that time of night, the resident's small bar.

From here Sid realised that his bedroom would have been almost directly overhead but the only noise coming from the bar was the low hum of chatter from those residents who hadn't retired to their rooms and a lot of swearing coming from his old colleague Mick who appeared to be loosing most of his weeks spending money on the one armed bandit in the corner.

Then, all of a sudden Sid heard the noise that had awoken him from his slumbers.

'What the hell is that' asked Sid of the barman who was pouring out a pint of Guinness for a little old lady who didn't look as if she could lift a pint glass let alone consume its contents.

'That bloody drumming noise.'

'Oh that sir. That's our skittle alley, second door on the left between the gent's toilets and the portrait of Neil Kinnock.'

Sid slowly opened the door to find himself at one end of a long corridor with a concrete floor. At the far end stood two men closely studying the position of a number of wooden pegs. Immediately in front of Sid were two other men one of whom was clutching a large wooden ball.

The men from the far end of the alley then walked back along it towards Sid, turned and then one of them launched the ball in the direction from which they had come towards the remaining upstanding skittles.

The noise to Sid was deafening as the solid wooden ball rolled along the concrete with the sound echoing around the narrow alleyway until it made contact with the wooden skittles and sent them in turn crashing against the back walls.

At this point the men noticed they had a visitor.

'Hello Sid, come to watch or play' enquired Eric a fellow traveller.

'Neither' responded Sid 'I came to see what all the racket was.'

'Yeah a bit noisy ain't it replied the man who had just bowled the ball but we aren't disturbing anyone down here are we?'

'Not disturbing anyone! My bloody bedroom is right above this alleyway. Nearly shook me out of me bed it did that bloody ball rolling down this concrete roadway.'

'Oh sorry Sid' they all responded we had no idea we were under someone's bedroom and besides I thought you were over the other side of the hotel with the sea view.' Got yourself a room next to Mrs Morgan!'

The players looked at one another and smiled. Sid did not see the funny side.

'Anyway Sid its only 9:30 bit early for bed on your holidays isn't it unless you and Mrs Morgan…'

He didn't have time to finish the sentence as Sid interjected that he had hardly seen her that holiday and that she appeared to be avoiding him for some reason.

'Ah playing hard to get hey' said Eric.

'Look, sod worrying about me and the widow and have more concern for someone trying, for the second night in a row, to get some sleep.'

Sid then explained his problems of the night before with the disco and that the hotel had agreed to move him to a quieter part of the hotel.

'Not having a peaceful break are we Sid' remarked Eric trying to hold back a smile.

'No I ain't and it doesn't help me standing here watching you four buggers having a good laugh at my expense'

'Sorry Sid' they all responded in unison we are nearly finished, should be clear of the alley in about 30 minutes.'

'Well thanks chaps I don't want to be a spoil sport coz you're all on your holidays too, but I would appreciate that.'

At that Sid turned and walked out of the door to the giggles of the men who could see his white pyjama cord extending out from the back of his trousers and trailing along behind him like some kind of tail.

As he closed the door behind him Sid glanced at the

notice pinned to it. It was advertising the next 'Inter Hotels and Pubs Skittles League match to be held the following evening at the St. Swithins Hotel between St Swithins Wanderers and The Talbut Inn Flyers.

The remainder of Sid's night was peaceful as, true to their word, the skittle alley fell silent about 20 minutes after he had returned to his room.

Next morning Sid again visited the reception of the hotel and it was again the unfortunate Carol who was sitting behind the desk.

'Good Morning, Mr. Saines isn't it?'

'No it's not and yes it is' replied Sid.

'I'm sorry but I don't understand.'

'Well that makes two of us then because I can't understand why after I complained about my noisy room on Saturday night you relocated me to one which was even worse.'

'I'm very sorry Mr Saines but I am quite sure you could not hear the Disco from your new room'

'It's not the sodding disco I'm talking about' shouted Sid beginning to loose his composure. 'It's your bloody skittle alley.'

'Oh I see, well what do you want me to do about it?'

'I want you to move me, that is what I want, retorted Sid.'

'Well I am very sorry but we do not have any spare rooms available, even the room you vacated yesterday is now occupied.'

'How the hell am I supposed to sleep then if that racket

of last night is to be a regular affair?'

'Well I am sorry you were disturbed last night but the alley and the bar to which it is attached is for residents only up to 11:00 pm and therefore it is unlikely that it will be used after that time given the nature of the residents we have in this week. Apart from your party Mr Saines, who I am sure are all tucked up in bed by that time of night like yourself, we have a small party of Franciscan Friars and six ladies attending the Alvin Stardust convention at the Conference Centre.'

'Well maybe the monks and the women might not be using the Alley but there are some blokes in my party that like a drop of beer and as they are on their holidays may not think that 11:00 is a suitable time for bed.'

'Well in that instance sir' the receptionist responded 'You will need to use your powers of persuasion on them because there is nothing more I can offer unless one of your colleagues in a double room wouldn't mind sharing'

'Don't you start; I've had enough from so called mates on that subject.'

The receptionist sat bemused as Sid turned to walk away with the passing comment

'We will see what tonight brings' as he disappeared towards the breakfast room and his appointment with a "Full English".

In the restaurant Sid settled back in a chair opposite Charlie, who had been one of the gang of four that had been in the alley the night before.

'Morning Charlie, did you enjoy the end of your game last night, you were true to your word, after about ten minutes I didn't hear a sound, got a good nights sleep after all.'

'Not really Sid, this weather is so un-seasonal and what with there being no form of heating in that bloody alley poor old Dickies fingers started turning blue and I think George has got a chill in his guts today. He spent most of the early hours of the morning on the bog and as he was too tight to pay for en-suite he has been creating a bit of a bottleneck with the bathroom at the end of the corridor, not to mention the inconvenience of him having to leg it down the corridor at regular intervals hoping that no one is in the toilet.

'It might have been the fish interjected Sid, it smelt a bit strong.'

'No I had that that and it ain't shifted me. Usual trouble I 'ave on holiday'

'Poor old George, looks like he hasn't managed to get down for breakfast because of his trouble and you know how much he likes his food.'

'Yeah' replied Sid picturing Dick the evening before in the alleyway, 'he certainly takes up a fair bit of room'. 'So you won't be playing skittles for a while then?'

'No chance Sid, too much like hard work all that walking up and down and standing the skittles up but its the bloody cold that gets you. Bet it's freezing down there even in a heat wave.'

Sid smiled to himself, well seems I ain't got too much to worry about on the late night skittles front he thought and he was right because for the rest of the holiday his nights were peaceful except for the occasional noise in the corridor of the unfortunate George making a hurried trip to the toilet. Even the scheduled inter hotel and pub match with the Talbut Flyers was cancelled due to 'holiday commitments' according to the scribbed sign Sid passed on the way out of the breakfast room.

As usual the days of Sid's annual holiday seemed to fly past. No sooner had he got up, washed and had breakfast than it seemed to be time to sit down for dinner. Sid always enjoyed the various excursions and this particular day the group were to visit Salisbury. He knew little about the town except that it had a cathedral and a number of old buildings.

The coach off-loaded its passengers in the coach park at 11:00 with the driver requesting everyone to be back by 3:30 sharp for the return journey to Bournemouth. Sid left the coach in the company of George, now fully recovered and Mrs. Morgan who appeared to have overcome her anger with Sid and his suggestions on cohabitation. The trio walked along the banks of the river towards the spire that dominated the town. This was the direction the driver had advised them to take as the shortest route to the town.

Once in the centre they went their separate ways as each had their own ideas of what they wanted to do. Mrs Morgan wanted to visit the market, Dickie had heard there was a local brewery and therefore decided to find a pub that stocked the local ale and Sid decided that he would like to visit the Cathedral.

Arriving at the main entrance after walking across the wide expanse of grass Sid was confronted with the sign requesting the payment of £3 as a donation for all visitors to the building. Sid was never easily parted from his money and begrudged having to pay for anything particularly as he thought it was only a large church and that it should be free to enter a place of worship. 'What if I don't want to make the recommended contribution' Sid asked the attendant at the desk.

'That's your prerogative sir, but I am sure you will appreciate it takes an awful lot of money for the upkeep of this magnificent building and that in order for people in the future to enjoy it we must maintain it.'

'I understand that,' replied Sid 'but pensioners like me can't afford £3 just to look round a church.'

'That's entirely up to you sir, if you feel that way please put any donation you feel applicable in the box on the wall as you enter.'

'Oh well thank you replied Sid as he withdrew some loose change from his pocket and dropped it into the receptacle.

Sid enjoyed his walk around the Cathedral to the extent that as he exited he put some more money into the box to equate to the £3 fee he had originally been asked for.

Once outside he looked up at the magnificent façade and the tallest spire in England, a fact he had gleaned from the free leaflet he had picked up at the City information Centre. As he stood gazing up it dawned on Sid that he was looking at the same building in the picture that he had often admired which hung in the Cozy Café. Just wait until I tell old Cooper next time we meet thought Sid.

All too soon the holiday was over and as he and his fellow travellers returned north and home with their acquaintenships renewed they promised to keep in touch though out the year. A promise none of them would keep.

Arriving back at his bungalow Sid waved to the

passengers still left on the coach as it drew away and opened his front door to be confronted with an array of bills and circulars laying on his mat and a friendly welcome home rub around his legs by Fluff.

Chapter 18

It was a Thursday morning and Sid sat in his favourite armchair reading his local newspaper. There is less and less news in this bloody rag nowadays he murmured to himself, all it contains is bloody adverts for new conservatories, houses for sale or how badly the local football team are doing and advocating that the manager or the board should be sacked. It was at that moment, as Sid was reading that his local council were intending to introduce Parking Wardens to the town's High Street to control the ad hoc parking that he noticed that a familiar car had pulled up outside his house. It was a royal blue Skoda being driven by his son Mark.

It was very unusual for him to arrive unannounced. In fact it was rare for him to arrive at all and so it was with a mixture of apprehension as to why he was calling and pleasure to see him that Sid greeted him on his front step.

'Hi dad' said Mark 'Nice to see you. Your looking well but still not given up those bloody fags I see'. Mark had always complained about his dad's addiction to smoking and had long since realised that wild horses wouldn't stop him but that didn't prevent him making pointed comments at every opportunity on his fathers habit and particularly about the damage it was doing to his health.

'My father smoked from the age of twelve' Sid retorted as the two of them went through the usual ritual. 'And he lived to 92 so it didn't do him a lot of harm.

Mark had heard all the excuses before and so just shrugged his shoulders and walked into the familiar chill that was his father's bungalow. Sid wouldn't use the gas fire unless it was absolutely necessary. After having his usual lecture on smoking and not keeping himself warm enough Sid asked to what did he deserve the honour of his visit.

Mark then explained that he and his wife had recently purchased a property in France and that they were going over in a few weeks time and wondered if Sid wanted to join them.

Sid was flabbergasted at the thought. Not only by being invited on holiday with his son and daughter-in-law but also that they had bought a place in France.

'Are you sure about this' asked Sid.

'Sure about what dad?'

'This place abroad you've got. I've seen a lot of programmes on television about people getting caught buying these Time Share places and being ripped off.'

'Its okay dad' replied Mark. 'It's our house, not a time share, all legally done through solicitors just like buying a house in England.'

Sid was still not convinced but was by now becoming more interested in the fact that he was going to get a foreign holiday.

'Where is the place then' enquired Sid. 'Down on the

Riviera, Nice or somewhere like that?'

'No dad it's in Brittany near Dinan.'

Sid had heard of Brittany but he had no idea where in France it was, let alone the town of Dinan.

'Look' said Mark, getting a map out of his pocket. 'Here is England okay and here is Portsmouth.'

'I bloody know where Portsmouth is' replied Sid indignantly.

Mark ignored him and continued.

'Well if you look due south from here you hit the northern coast of France and Normandy.'

'I've heard of Normandy' said Sid. 'That's where the beaches are that the allied troop landed on in 1945.'

'Correct dad, and if you go west along the Normandy coast the next province you meet is Brittany, famous for its cider, pancakes seafood and everything Breton.'

'Well I like a drop of cider and me pancakes with syrup and winkles so that sounds all okay to me Mark.'

'Good, well Maria and I are going over by ferry on the Thursday and we thought you might like to come. I know you and mum had a passport years ago when you went to Belgium but you probably need to renew it.' Sid got up from his armchair and walked across to the sideboard. After a few minutes of rifling through piles of papers and buff coloured envelopes he emerged triumphant with a navy blue passport in his hand. He opened it and peered into its contents but as he did not have his reading glasses on he was unable to decipher any dates within it. He passed the book to his son who quickly confirmed that he would need to renew it as it had expired eight years ago. The photograph also made Mark smile as it showed his father with a full head of hair and mutton chop side burns which had long since been replaced by a clean-shaven balding man.

'Do you want to come dad coz if so I need to make arrangements about the ferry and accommodation on it'

'Yeah sure I would like to come, but how long are we going for?'

'Only a week dad as I cant get any more time off work, but we thought you might like to come as we know how much you like pottering around and as it is an old house with lots of odd jobs which need doing we thought that you would be in your element.'

Hello, thought Sid, here is the ulterior motive for my invitation, there is work to be done and good old dad can be the cheap labour.

So what thought Sid, it would be a break from this house and Maria's a good cook so I will get well fed. Although, hang on a bit, I don't want any of that strange foreign grub.

'Aye Mark what about the food over there. Its not all frog's legs and snails is it?'

'No dad, I told you the region we are going to specialises in seafood, especially shrimps and shell fish and there is also the savoury pancakes with almost whatever filling you want.'

'You mean like Tate & Lyles Golden Syrup?'

'No dad, they have fillings like ham and eggs or mushrooms with garlic butter'. Then he thought for a moment 'Well they do have sweet pancakes as well for desert but I have never seen them with syrup. Sugar maybe,

153

and cream and a variety of fruit. All of this can be washed down with local Cider or strong black coffee just as you like it if you wish.'

'Well all right then responded Sid but just make sure if we go out to eat anywhere you don't order me something that was earlier that day hopping or slithering around. Okay.'

'Now we have got that clear dad do you want to come or not'

'How am I going to get there'?

'Look, I will collect you in the car' replied Mark beginning to regret he ever made the suggestion of his father coming to France.

'We will drive down to Portsmouth or Poole and get the lunchtime ferry on the Thursday. Don't worry about cost because we will pay, all you will need is your Euros for spending money and maybe a few tools we can put in the boot along with your suitcase'

'Okay then, I will come. How can I renew me passport?'

Mark explained that he would need to get a form from the post office and a new set of photographs and send them off with a cheque to the Regional Passport office, which he thought was in Preston.

'Look dad I have to go because I have a meeting. Maria will be pleased you are coming and I will telephone you next week to confirm arrangements. Meanwhile, don't forget to sort out your passport. Oh and get an E111 while your in the post office.'

With that Mark was gone and as the clatter of the Skoda's diesel engine slowly disappeared into the distance Sid was left standing on his doorstep thinking, well, a trip to France eh, that will be something for me to talk to old Cooper about next time we meet.

Sid turned and walked back into his house and then thought to himself, E111, I've heard about bloody e numbers but I thought they were food additives or colouring like blue Smarties, not something you got in the post office.

Next morning Sid made his way along the familiar footway to the town centre with the Post Office being his destination. As he strolled along carefully avoiding the deposits of the local dogs Sid began to recall his only other venture abroad with his wife and wondered if they had topless bathing in Dinan, or wherever it was they were going.

On reaching the town centre Sid crossed the busy High Street using the pedestrian crossing and was part the way across when a large white transit van, with a squeal of brakes, pulled up narrowly avoiding him.

Sid leapt to one side and then stood there and glowered at the driver and uttered a few well-chosen expletives in his direction. At that the driver lowered his window, stuck out his not inconsiderable sized head complete with a cigarette stuck to his bottom lip and gave Sid an equally eloquent reply.

'You bloody old fool, are you trying to get yourself killed, you just stepped right out onto the crossing without looking.' Sid walked up to the van, his composure returned after the initial shock, and stared at the driver. He was, Sid guessed in his late fifties, clean-shaven with a black cap and a protruding stomach that appeared to touch the steering wheel.

'If you had been paying attention', Sid responded, 'you would have seen me on the crossing a lot earlier and taken the appropriate action. Don't you know your highway code. You have to give way to us pedestrians on a zebra crossing?'

'Yeah, well I would but you have to give us a fighting chance. We can't be bloody mind readers. Pedestrians have a duty of care you know. You just bloody stepped out. Lucky I was alert.'

The two combatants then exchanged a few more words of abuse before Sid declared he had more important matters to attend to and with a final 'get stuffed' he walked away from the van, stood on the footway and waved a finger of defiance as the grime covered white van drew slowly away. At this point Sid noted that the van had the logo Igloo Secondary Windows emblazoned across it rear doors. Bloody double glazing contractor he thought. I might have guessed from his feisty attitude. Sid then smiled as he read, scrawled in the dirt on the back of the van 'I wish my wife was as dirty as this.'

Sid collected the appropriate forms his son had told him to get from the post office. He now knew that the E111 was a form needed to get reciprocal national health care when in an EU country, but was confused as to how he had to fill it in. Still he thought I could always pop up the local Citizens Advice Bureau to get help.

He then visited the local Woolworth's where he knew there was a passport photograph machine and, after enlisting some help from a female assistant who was replenishing the various receptacles on the pick and mix display, successfully achieved 4 photographs. He thought they made him look older than he was but he was not willing to spend any more money on further attempts to improve the quality of the machines output.

Armed with his photographs and forms Sid then headed for his local CAB office.

This was housed in a prefabricated building and accessed through the car park of the local council offices. Having visited the bureau a couple of times before Sid knew how helpful the staff there could be and that on a Friday they were open until five o'clock. On entering the building Sid found himself in a small room with about half a dozen chairs set around the outside. In one corner was a table on which were a number of magazines and leaflets explaining the work of the CAB and a collecting box with the words 'All Donations Welcome' emblazoned on the side. In the opposite corner of the room was a small desk with a telephone and computer behind which Sid could just make out the figure of a woman. He walked across to the desk to be greeted by a petite woman of around thirty, wearing a neat trouser suit and with her hair pulled back in a tight bun giving her already sharp features an even more piercing prominence.

'Good afternoon sir, can we help you?'

'Yes' responded Sid, pleased to be greeted in such a manner. Not like the receptionist down at the doctor's surgery he thought.

Sid explained his problem to the woman who listened attentively and confirmed that they would be pleased to help him but that unfortunately all of their trained advisers were currently with other clients but that as soon as one became available he would be seen to.

Sid sat in the waiting room for about ten minutes flicking through a copy of Hello Magazine and wondering how some of the women in the pictures managed not to fall out of their frocks. He was just beginning to read an article on the ratings wars between Coronation Street and Eastender's when a woman, who introduced herself as Daphne Smythe approached him. She had just completed dealing with a client who was facing eviction from his council house, had county court judgements against him and a habitual drug dependency problem, as well as severe halitosis.

It was, therefore, with some relief that she found that all Sid wanted was help in completing his E111 form and an application to renew his passport.

Within a quarter of an hour of entering the interview room Sid had completed his forms and had the relevance of the E111 form explained to him in layman's terms. He thanked Daphne as he left and put 50p into the collection box as he left. He had one outstanding need in respect of his passport and that was to get it duly authorised by a professional person who knew him. Dr Turner he thought.

As Sid walked away from the CAB offices he mused, now all I need is to get myself some of those Euros and I will be ready. He took the familiar walked back down the hill from the Council Offices to his bungalow.

Chapter 19

The day of Sid's departure for France dawned bright but with a chill in the air and the smell of freshly baked bread wafting along the street from the family bakers, Munday's, on the corner.

Sid had packed his suitcase the previous evening and so was ready and waiting and a little anxious by the time Mark arrived at 9:00 to collect him.

The journey southward was relatively uneventful. Sid had taken his car travel sickness pills and Mark's wife Maria had let him sit in the front passenger seat as Sid claimed that sitting in the back made him feel even more nauseous.

As he was not permitted to smoke in the car, to help counter his craving for something in his mouth Sid sucked a procession of extra strong mints. By the time the party reached Fleet Services on the M3 for one of the regular comfort break, the air in the car positively reeked of peppermint.

During the walk across the car park Sid explained to his son the methodology he adopted when buying a cup of tea in this particular type of establishment. Typical thought

Maria, although she couldn't stop smiling to herself. 'Well dad' responded Mark after he had listened to his fathers 'handy hints for travellers' we won't be stopping for tea. That hold up on the M25 has meant that we are running a bit late and we need to press on to the port.'

'That's okay by me I ain't thirsty at the moment. Let's push on.'

The three arrived at Portsmouth 45 minutes before sailing. They presented their documents at the check-in and then lined up in readiness to be directed onto the harbour side of embarkation. However, when the time came to move off they were directed towards the customs shed by an officious looking woman with a peaked cap and a dark official looking uniform with the words HM Customs written in gold lettering oh her applets. Once in the shed the travellers were approached by a tall bearded official who asked Mark to turn off his engine and proceeded to ask a number of questions.

'Did you pack the car yourself sir?'

'Yes', replied Mark.

'Are you the owner of this vehicle?'

'No, I am the legal keeper but it is a company car.'

'Thank you sir can you tell me the purpose of your trip and if you are carrying any sharp implements likes scythes or knives or any weapons.'

'No, only gardening implements and a few tools for running repairs on the house we have recently purchased in Brittany.'

'Now sir would you mind releasing the catch on the bonnet and the boot just so I can satisfy myself.'

Mark duly obliged and was about to get out of the car to add further assistance to the official when Sid piped up from the front seat.

'What the hell is he looking for,' enquired Sid in his best playground voice that reverberated throughout the echoing confines of the metal clad shed.

'Shush' said Maria, but it was obvious his comments had been heard.

Putting his head through the open car window the customs officer looked directly at Sid and said

'I am looking sir, for anything that you might have in the car that you should not be permitted to take either on board the ferry or into France.'

'Oh,' replied Sid I am sure we ain't. Do we look like smugglers? Besides I thought that people tried to smuggle things out of France not into it.'

'You would be surprised sir at what we sometimes find people trying to get out of the country.'

'Well we ain't trying to get away with anything' continued Sid unless you class my PG Tips and marmalade as smuggling and another thing…'

'Dad, just give over' whispered Maria into his ear from the back seat,' give it a rest.'

However as Sid could still hear the official moving boxes and bags around in the boot he couldn't stop himself.

'You see on the news all the people bringing in these druggy things into the country and there's these bloody officials asking us questions as if we were bloody criminals. Pity they can't be more thorough on stopping and searching the real smugglers.'

Suddenly there was a tap on the side window of the car. Sid turned to see the face of the Customs officer looking in and gesticulating with his index finger that he wanted Sid to get out of the car.

Sid unclipped his seatbelt and got out of the vehicle.

'Yes!'

'You are clearly unhappy with what we are doing sir and consider that you are above the law when it comes to matters of customs and excise.'

Before Sid could answer or try to defend his position he found that another officer was standing at his side.

'Will you please identify any of your belongings in the boot sir, or in the cabin of the car.'

Sid suddenly realised that maybe he had been a little over zealous in his condemnation of the customs officials but walked round to the back of the car and duly pointed out the beige holdall and deep red suitcase that he had brought with him.

The identified items were then removed from the car and taken to the side of the shed, they were then placed on a large trestle table and Sid was asked to open them.

The contents were then spread out for the entire world to view.

Sid's overalls and pyjamas and vests were set out alongside indigestion tablets, a torch, radio and various other items of clothing. The holdall contained a number of tools including screwdrivers, hammers and various tubs within which were all manner of nails and screws of varying size and head type.

'Thank you sir you may now put them back, I hope you

have a good holiday'

By the time Sid had repacked his bags and Mark had rearranged the boot to accommodate it they found that they were the last to leave the quayside and so once on board were at the back of the regimented rows of cars on the upper deck.

For the next few hours the atmosphere between Sid and his son and daughter-in-law was a bit frosty. Due to their delay in getting on board they found themselves almost at the back of the queue for the on board cafeteria and so not only did they have to wait an inordinately long time to get served but also found that by the time they reached the service counter that most of the popular meals were sold out. Fortunately for Sid the sea crossing for the 5 hour journey was smooth and once he had availed himself of the duty free shop and purchased his packets of Old Holborn he found that the journey passed quite pleasantly.

By the time they docked in Cherbourg everyone's temper had mellowed but as they drove off the ferry Mark turned to his father.

'Now dad not a word, okay, as we go through customs alright?'

'All right son, I've learnt me lesson but those Frenchies wouldn't be able to understand me would they.'

'Don't be too sure dad. They are mostly bilingual and they have even less of a sense of humour than their colleagues back in England.'

Sid nodded ruefully and true to his word he remained silent until they were clear of the port and driving up the hill out of Cherbourg and heading south.

Chapter 20

The two and a half hour journey was a relatively quiet affair with the sound of Radio Nostalgique only being interrupted by Sid's utterings in respect of some piece of scenery he had just spotted or a road sign.

'We've just gone through Saint Lo' he observed 'never heard of him, wonder what he might be patron saint of?'

Over the years Mark and Maria had come to ignore, to a great extent, what Sid said and today was no exception. They continued to listen to the local radio station and with their limited knowledge of French tried to deduce what was being said between the record tracks. It was dark by the time they reached their destination. The car headlamps briefly scanned the front of the cottage as the vehicle swung onto the short driveway before coming to rest pointing directly at the front door. Sid had been shown photographs of the house before but was surprised at its size and the sense of presence that its granite blocks gave it.

Mark hurried round to the side of the house and opened up the meter box and dropped the switch to turn the electricity on. He then opened up the door of the boiler shed, turned on the water supply and then the oil-fired boiler. After a short delay it fired up and he returned to the front of the house.

'Home at last' sighed Maria who was treating Sid as a roundabout whilst she traipsed back and forward from the car in the dark with Sid seemingly transfixed standing in the driveway looking round at his different surroundings.

'Bloody dark here ain't it' said Sid.

'Yes dad, you're in the country now or on the edge of a village at least.'

The few streetlights that there are here are switched off at 10:30. Sid had lived for so long in the town with its street lighting glare that he had forgotten just how dark the countryside could be and how bright and numerous the stars were in the night sky in an area not polluted with artificial light. He eventually realised that he was becoming a hindrance and began to help unpack the car. Soon they were all inside the cottage which Sid noted was open plan on the ground floor with the kitchen to the right of the main entrance door as you entered and the lounge area to the left. There was a toilet and bathroom off the kitchen and an oak staircase going straight up out of the centre of the room.

Sid mounted the stairs, which twisted half way up and, from a small landing, opened a door into a bedroom that was about the size of his entire bungalow back home in Creekleigh. Bugger me he thought this is a big room. He looked round and saw it contained 3 beds. A double and two singles. Oh, oh, he thought we are all going to have to sleep in the same room. I don't much fancy that. But at that moment Sid heard the sound of a door opening and he turned to see Mark coming out of an adjoining room. Sid walked across to the door and peered into the chamber.

There he saw another room just as large as the one he was standing in.

'Like a bloody tardis this place ain't it son' he said.

'Yes dad, it's quite spacious.'

'I thought I was going to have to sleep with you and Maria when I saw the size of this room and the three beds in it'

'No fear dad, I don't think that would suit any of us do you?'

Father and son smiled at each other and went downstairs, as they were being summoned by Maria who declared that a cup of tea was on the table. A little bit of England in France thought Sid as he sipped his PG Tips and looked around at his surroundings.

As Sid laid down that evening he reflected on his day and hoped that Maria and Mark had forgiven him for the trouble at the Port that morning and vowed that, whilst in their company at least he would not let his inbuilt anathema to authority manifest itself in such a strident way.

Sid sat up in bed with a start, totally disorientated as one is on waking up in strange surroundings and in an unfamiliar bed. What the hell is that he thought to himself as through his partially opened bedroom window came the sound of tolling bells. He looked across the gloom of his bedroom towards his trusty travel alarm clock that had accompanied him over many holidays in recent years. Six o'clock he muttered to himself, six o'clock he repeated. I know we are in the country and country folk like to get up with the lark but this is taking the piss. Those bells must wake the whole village. After what seemed like an eternity the bells stopped but by this time Sid was wide awake and so decided to get up and go downstairs to make the household an early morning cup of tea.

Sid tried to creep down the old wooden staircase but it creaked and groaned with his every movement.

Once in the green walled kitchen, all the walls were green, Sid duly made a pot of tea and whilst waiting for it to brew decided to have a look at the garden that he had been unable to do in the dark on his arrival the previous evening. It was also the opportunity for him to have a cigarette as he was banned from smoking in the house. Sid could not venture too far as he was still in his dressing gown but as he stepped out of the back door of the cottage he was confronted with a relatively compact patio and grassed area about thirty feet long with a green painted shed at the end of it. It had a hedge along one side and a raised border to the opposite side. Well thought Sid this is not too bad, a bit of straightening up of the edges of the grass and getting some weeds out of the flower bed should be dead easy.

Sid finished his roll-up and went back into the house, poured the tea, placed the cups on a tray and ascended the stairs.

To get to his son's room Sid had to pass through his own. The interconnecting door had frosted glass in the top half and through it Sid was able to detect that there was no movement in the room beyond it.

Sid knocked loudly on the door and was greeted with a dozy 'Yeah, okay.'

Sid entered the room and put the tray down on the table at the foot of the bed and was about to leave when his son enquired if he slept well.

'Yeah' replied Sid 'But those bloody church bells ringing

at six in the morning ain't my idea of being woken gently.'

'What do you mean six dad, the church bell in the village is sounded every day at 7am, 7pm and midday. You must still be operating on English time. They are one hour ahead of us here you know, didn't you hear them making announcements on the ferry on the way over. They use English time on board but the timetable are all related to local times.'

'Oh right' exclaimed Sid. 'But ain't it still a bit early?'

'You get used to it dad and either take account of it or ignore it.'

'Oh by the way' said Sid 'I have had a look at the garden, not too much to do is there, but the grass cutting and a bit of edging should see it okay'.

'I am impressed dad, I found the garden a daunting prospect, it took me and Peter two days just to cut all the grass when we first bought the house.

'What' exclaimed Sid, 'It must have been in a hell of a state to take the two of you that long, but you have certainly got it round.'

'Got it round! I only wish I had, just look at it.'

Mark got out of bed and pulled back the curtains.

'Look dad' he gesticulated towards the window, 'do you really think that I've got this garden in any sort of order?'

Sid did as he was bid and looked out of the window and down into the garden below.

Mark could see the direction of his fathers gaze and suddenly realised that he had not appreciated what was beyond the shed. 'No dad' he said. 'Look up, look beyond the green shed. Sid gazed up and staring beyond the shed was, he estimated, another 200 feet plus of rough grass, interspersed with fruit trees and shrubs. 'Yes dad, that is also the garden, the bit from the house to the shed is simply just the part we have managed to get to grips with. We were hoping you might be able to help us with the bit beyond it.'

'Bugger me' said Sid. 'We are only here for a week, it would take me months to get that lot sorted out'

'Yeah I know dad, but anything you can do to make inroads on the area would be greatly appreciated.'

Sid shrugged his shoulders, promised to see what he could do and left his son to his early morning tea. On going downstairs Sid decided to take advantage of the vacant bathroom and had a wash and shave. He was surprised to find that the water was hot and plentiful and that the loo flushed okay. He had heard a lot of stories about French plumbing. As Sid was coming out of the bathroom Mark was descending the stairs.

'We need to get some fresh bread and croissants for breakfast dad. As you are up and dressed do you want to pop down to the patisserie and get them?'

'Oh I don't know about that Mark, I can't speak the lingo you know that.'

'That's not a problem dad, all you have to say is une baguette et trois croissants sil vous plait. I will write it down for you and if you want you can just hand it over to the shop assistant. It will cost no more than five Euros and so just give the woman in the shop the money, she's a lovely lady, and that's it.'

'I'm not sure son but if you say so I'll give it a go.'

'I suggest you take my bike out the shed dad, that way you will be a lot quicker, meanwhile I'll set the breakfast table.'

After confirming precisely where the patisserie was and being advised that in such a small village, with only one main street, it would be difficult to miss, Sid set off on Mark's bike.

On entering the shop Sid was immediately impressed with the quality of the cakes that were on display and the friendliness in the way he was greeted by the lady behind the counter. Looking down at his instructions Sid tried to repeat what was written on it but despite his best efforts there was just a blank expression on the face of the assistant who smiled sympathetically and held out her hand.

Sid duly passed Mark's note and the five euros over. She nodded in recognition and handed Sid the three croissants along with a baguette and 20 cents change.

She then wished Sid 'Bon journey'. Sid responded with 'Thank you' and walked out of the shop.

The next problem was getting the bread home. Sid had bought a carrier bag for the croissants which he hung over the handlebars, but when he placed the baguette into the bag it was too long and kept threatening to topple out. He then had what he thought was a brilliant idea. At the back of the bike was a pannier with a spring-loaded clip. He decided that if he was careful he could put the baguette at right angles to the bike, and then gently lower the clip over it thereby securing it to the bike. This he duly did, but as he scooted away from the shop and swung his leg over the saddle it caught the projecting loaf causing it to be snapped off with the detached portion falling off and rolling into the village street.

Bugger, thought Sid, as he jumped off his bike and retrieved the muddied end of the baguette. Now what do I do? Sid was in quandary. Did he return to the house minus half the loaf or return to the patisserie and get another? He decided that he had let down his son the day before and should replace the loaf, but he was gripped with fear of asking for another in the shop.

Sid parked his bike and re-entered the shop. He was greeted with a friendly smile that helped to put him more at ease. He placed two euros on the counter and pointed to the rack of bread behind the still smiling woman. Fortunately for Sid the woman appeared to understand his gesticulations and removed a baguette and held it in front of her. Sid nodded in acceptance. The loaf was wrapped, change was handed over and Sid left the premises with a 'Thank ya' to which a bon journee was the response. Madam Guillame and her husband had, unknown to Sid, observed the entire episode of his snapping the baguette. The baker and she had had great difficulty in not laughing at Sid as he had returned for a replacement loaf.

On his return to the house Sid related the tale and with pride explained that unaided and without the aid of a safety net he had made himself understood in the shop and eventually acquired the required goods. His next encounter with a French woman would be far less conducive.

That evening Sid was introduced to the neighbours Tiery and Marie. He was a retired electrician and his wife was still employed as a schoolteacher at a local primary school. Fortunately Tiery had a good grasp of English although he had some difficulty in cutting through Sid's heavy accent. Tiery was a very good neighbour to Mark and Maria. He kept a watchful eye on their house in their absence and made sure that in the winter the frost stat of the boiler kept the property safe from freezing.

During the journey to the cottage Mark had explained to Sid that the roof was in need of repair and that they were going to talk to the neighbour to discuss what options he could suggest. Earlier that day Sid had ventured into the loft, which had a vast space, and noted through the gloom that there were shafts of sunlight that were shining through gaps in the slates leaving bright spots of light on the floorboards. There was also a bucket in the corner in which Sid had noted was a couple of inches of water.

'What do you suggest we do about the roof Tiery?' asked Mark.

'Well I have been thinking mon ami and I believe you have three possible options.'

'You can continue patching up the roof as your predecessor Madam Lafaite did. That way you may get another two years out of it. Alternatively you could see about getting a local builder to do the work. I could see if any of my friends know who might be able to help.'

'And the third option 'asked Sid.

'Well, when I moved into my house it was only a shell and I employed an architect from Dinan who appointed the contractors and oversaw the work.'

'Seems a bit of overkill,' said Sid. 'You don't need an architect to put slates on a roof.'

'Maybe dad, but don't forget we are not very good at the language and having the roof off is a pretty fundamental venture. Could you make sure they kept to a schedule and that the work was done to French building standards'

Sid shrugged his shoulders.

'It's your money son.'

They agreed to think it over and on that note Tiery shook the men's hands, kissed Maria on both cheeks and made his departure, clutching the bottle of malt whiskey that he had been given for his work on looking after the house.

The following morning dawned bright and clear and after breakfast Mark announced that they were going to see some friends who had recently bought a holiday house in Comborg and by coincidence they were also in residence that week. Sid felt that he would be intruding if he went and so suggested he could maybe do a few odd jobs whilst they were away.

After some debate it was agreed that the upstairs windows at the front of the house would benefit from some fresh paint.

After retrieving the grey paint from the loft and an appropriate sized brush, father and son studied the window and discussed the best way to prepare and paint it.

Sid was given some sandpaper and a cloth and advised by Mark that the French name for a window was 'fenetre.'

'Fenetra' repeated Sid.

'That's close enough dad, we will see you in a couple of hours. If you need to make yourself a drink you know where the stuff is, and if you have to go out make sure you lock up. I've got a spare key so don't worry'.

Chapter 21

Sid picked up a piece of medium grade sandpaper and began to rub down the window frame. The paint began to fall off in large flakes and revealed a multitude of colours that, over time, had been the choice of the various house owners. Been some time since this old bit of wood saw a lick of paint he thought as the dust mingled with the cigarette ash that dropped from the roll-up. Sid was not supposed to smoke in the house but he thought that as he was by an open window the smoke fumes would go outside and not affect the home. He was to be proved wrong.

As he rubbed away there was the occasional passer by who greeted him with a bonjour to which Sid responded happily but was equally pleased that the bearers of the greetings continued walking and did not attempt to engage him in conversation.

Sid was about to roll himself another cigarette when his attention was drawn to an elderly lady with a small mongrel dog who had suddenly appeared, standing on the edge of the roadway and gesticulating with a jabbing forefinger towards him.

'Monsieur, monsieur' she began.

'Eer yeah, bonjour madam' responded Sid who continued to construct his cigarette and ignore the old woman. Unfortunately she was not to be disregarded. Her apparent gabbling became more intense as she firstly pointed up towards the roof of the house and then down to the spot she was standing on. Sid did not have the faintest of ideas of what the old dear was saying but he eventually deduced from her mannerism and gesticulations that she was continuing to point to the roof and that she also wanted him to come down.

It was now that Sid noted she was also pointing across the village towards the church and muttering the words fenetre and toit. Sid then remembered that from the conversation they had had with the neighbour the day before these were French for window and roof.

So it began to dawn on Sid that maybe the old woman had some knowledge of the fact that his son wanted a new roof. A chance to redeem myself thought Sid. If I could sort something out for him then it might go some way to appeasing the two of them for my cock up on the ferry.

As Sid stood beside the old lady in the road outside of the house, she continued to point up towards the roof of the dwelling and then in the direction of the church and began to tug at his sleeve. She clearly wants me to go with her thought Sid, well here goes I might learn something for Mark about the local builder, even if it's only where he lives.

'Come on then missus' said Sid quite forgetting for the moment the nationality of the woman.

The pair then set off at a brisk walking pace with the old dear still rabbiting away to Sid and him responding with yeah's and okay.

During their walk through the village the couple did not encounter a single soul. It was as if the whole place was deserted or that people were hiding away. As they rounded the corner of the main street the woman waved her hand in the direction of what Sid thought were three or four terraced houses where a man was standing in the garden of one reciprocating the wave.

As they drew closer the waves between the two became more intense and Sid could see that the man was in his twenties, heavily set and standing by a ladder, which appeared to reach up to the roof of the house.

Ah thought Sid my idea was right, he is clearly a builder and doing some work on the old dears' roof. Its marvellous how the old jungle telegraph works, we had only been talking about a possible job twenty-four hours ago. However Sid's notion was about to be scotched. On entering through the garden gate the dog that had dutifully followed the pair to the house went ballistic. It chased up and down the small garden barking and jumping up at Sid.

Eventually the man Sid had identified as a builder removed his beret and took a swipe at the mutt which whimpered and walked dejectedly towards the only tree in the garden, sat down under it and began licking those parts male dogs tend to lick.

As Sid walked towards the house the man held out his hand and shook Sid's warmly. He then noticed that the ladder did not go to the roof of the house but only as far as an open first floor window. At the same time he also noticed a large double divan bed frame at the foot of the ladder. Through a series of gesticulation Sid soon realised that his idea of making an initial contact with a builder for his son was not to materialise. Instead, he found himself helping the man (who subsequently turned out to be the old woman's son) get the bed through the first floor window via an ancient and rickety wooden ladder. What followed was pure farce.

The two men grappled with the bed and with it resting on their shoulders they commenced to climb up part of the ladder and then use its angle against the house wall to push it towards the open window.

Once a critical point had been reached the son supporting the bed on his shoulder despatched Sid into the house.

Guided by the old woman Sid climbed the old wooden staircase, which clearly was of an inadequate width and alignment to permit large furniture to pass up or down it, and entered a small bedroom that had a lingering aroma of stale foot odour.

Sid leaned out of the large bedroom window and, with the mother and neurotic dog alongside, waited whilst the son hoisted the bed the final distance so that Sid could grasp a corner and begin to haul it in. With the bed balanced and the windowsill forming a fulcrum the son left his duties on the ladder and took over from his mother inside the bedroom to help guide the piece of furniture over its last few metres.

To this day Sid can still recall the smell of the body odour of the old woman combined with that coming from the dirty white trainers on the bedroom floor and the breathe of the dog as it, with its front paws on the open window frame panted in excitement. Once the bed was safely hauled in the son gesticulated that it had to be placed in the adjacent room. This was carried out relatively simply and at the end of the exercise Sid was ushered downstairs

177

and offered a drink from a bottle which contained a clear liquid that appeared to have the consistency of used motor oil but without the colour. Sid politely refused the offer of his hosts and with that both members o   f the family shook his hand rigorously, expressed their gratitude again and led him to the front door.

Sid walked up the path of the house with the dog still sniffing at his ankles. He closed the gate, turned and gave a farewell wave to the couple and strolled slowly back to his sons' house rolling a cigarette as he went and thinking what an introduction he was having to French life.

As Sid passed between the cottages he could not help but notice that there appeared to be more people on the streets and he thought to himself, that old dear must have walked about half a mile through the village before she got to me, strange that she didn't meet someone else in all that distance!!

By coincidence, as Sid reached the house his son and daughter-in-law were also just returning from their visit to their friends.'

'Hi dad' exclaimed Mark as he got out of the car 'Finished the windows and been for a constitutional and a fag around the village then. Met a nice widowed madam.'

'No, on all counts,' came the reply from Sid who immediately set about recounting his tale of the old woman, his misconception of what she had wanted and his labours that afternoon on a ladder and in her boudoir. By the time he had completed his tale all three of them were grinning. 'Sounds like a bit of a caper from Last of the Summer Wine dad.'

'Aye son, with me and my old painting clothes on and the

old dear with her long skirt and cardigan we must have looked a bit like Compo and Nora Batty.'

Over the course of the days Sid and Mark had collected a number of bags of rubbish both from the garden in terms of cuttings, grass and weeds along with cardboard and items that were still being found in the loft left by the previous occupants. As a result of this Mark studied the details he had obtained from his neighbour on the days and times of opening of the Civic amenity site in nearby Dinan. It was only open to the public alternate days, excluding weekends, but fortunately that day was one when it was scheduled to be open. Worse than back home in Creekleigh thought Sid as Mark explained the timetable to him over a mug of PG Tips.

The two of them loaded up the car and headed out of the village and onto the dual carriageway towards Dinan. The journey was only a few kilometres and so there was not time for Sid to light up a cigarette, albeit Mark would have stopped him anyway. On arrival at the tip they followed the signs to the area set aside for vegetation and disposed of the contents of the main sacks and then drove through to the main body of the 'dechetterie', as Sid noticed it was called from the signs on the main gate and the site operatives hut.

'Bit like back home ain't it Mark' remarked Sid as the car passed between the various skips festooned with various descriptions of what was and wasn't permitted to be placed within them. Mark however, was not listening as he had glanced out of the corner of his eye that a man in navy blue overalls with a cigarette hanging from the corner of his mouth had watched their entry through the gate from the doorway of the site hut and was walking towards the slow moving car.

As Mark espied a receptacle displaying the words BOIS he stopped the car and got out. Unaware of what Mark had been observing Sid also alighted from the vehicle and was immediately confronted by the Frenchman who rattled off at great speed a torrent of words, none of which Sid understood but from the tone Sid thought that they were not words of greeting.

'What's he on about Mark?' asked Sid looking to his son for some kind of explanation.

'I am not sure dad, he's speaking so fast and I have trouble with the language when it's delivered slowly.'

The site operative soon realised that even by shouting he was not getting through to the English couple and so reverted to the tried and trusted sign language and gesticulations. He beckoned Mark and Sid to follow him to another car parked a few metres away and then pointed to the cars windscreen. There in the bottom right hand corner was a small round disc on which was printed a blue and white abstract symbol and the words 'DECHETTERIE PASS.'

The man then walked back to their car, pointed at the windscreen and shook his head.

'What's the bloke on about' asked Sid.

'Seems as if we haven't got permission to tip here dad, we haven't got an official sticker.'

Father and son were then signalled to open up the boot of their car to reveal what it was they had brought to the site to dispose of. Mark duly did as he was bid and revealed 3 plastic sacks containing a mixture of cardboard and wood off-cuts.

The man in overalls who had now been joined by a colleague, who Sid thought looked like a Youth Opportunities Trainee, gesticulated to a couple of skips that Mark had already identified for use and then proceeded to watch as father and son tipped their loads into the appropriate receptacles. As Mark got back into the car the two men approached the side door and again gave the two visitors a verbal assault from which Mark was able to extricate the words Mairee and Permit.

As they drove away Mark could see in his rear mirror that the younger of the two site operatives was writing something down in a notebook, which he assumed was his registration number whilst the older man was lighting another cigarette and striding off towards another tipper who was probably carrying out some other misdemeanour, which required his immediate attention.

'What was all that about Mark' asked Sid as they exited the gate and started heading back home.

'It seems dad that you can't just turn up and dispose of your household rubbish you need a permit which I deduce from our friend back there you get from the local Mairee or mayor'

'Officious little blighter wasn't he, mind you not a lot different to those down the tip back home in Creekleigh. They have the self-opinionated air that they are doing you a favour by allowing you to use the tip, but I have never been told I need a bloody permit. Fancy needing to have a badge to allow you to dump! Mark smiled.

'Well dad we will have to visit the Mairee's office in the village and see how we go about getting one of theses passes for the tip and obtain a permit otherwise we are going to have to run the gauntlet every time we go with Monsieur jobs worth. If experience of getting anything official in France is anything to go by we will probably have to fill in forms in triplicate, get proof of address and all documents countersigned by a witness.

The fact was that the next day Mark went to the Mairee's office and asked for a Dechetterie Pass and was immediately handed a self adhesive disc with no questions asked and no forms to fill in.

At first this had puzzled him because experience had taught him that bureaucracy was everything in France, along with proof of identity, but then he thought that as they were the only English people with a property in the village their presence and details were far better known than they realised and so the simple act of securing a permit was made far easier than it might have been.

By comparison the remainder of the week in France was relatively uneventful and so it was on the last evening of the week away that, to thank Sid for the hours he had put in trying to get the garden into some kind of order and not getting into any more scrapes with authority, they decided to take him out for evening dinner. The word evening being mentioned because as far as Sid was concerned dinner was at lunchtime and in the evening you had your tea or supper. On being told, Sid's initial reaction was somewhat reticent and on being prompted he confided that he was concerned he might not like the food and that he didn't want to upset them by doing so. Both Mark and Maria assured him that the food would not be a problem and that they knew how he liked his food, plain and plenty of it and that they knew a restaurant that would cater for his dietary requirements.

With Sid's acquiescence, that evening the three drove the

short distance into Dinan and then after parking in the town square they strolled into the heart of the old town. None of the trio liked eating late and so it was about 7:30 when they entered Le Cygne Restaurant.

Sid put his reading glasses on and stared at the menu.

'It's all in French,' he whispered to Maria, an event in itself for Sid to whisper anything, as she did not know he had a volume knob for his voice.

'Yes Dad.' she replied, 'We are in France, you would expect a menu in an English restaurant to be in English wouldn't you?'

'Well yes, but you said the food would be plain and simple, but this menu looks anything but. Here, what's this then' asked Sid his large knarled fore finger pointing to a dish part way down the menu. 'Dinde, what the hell is dinde'?

'It's turkey dad.'

'Well what's this then' he again asked 'Legumes.'

'They are vegetables dad.'

'What sort?'

'Just vegetables.'

'Look at this,' he suddenly shouted.

'Shush dad' responded Maria, realising the whispering phase was too good to last. 'Look at what dad.'

'This' said Sid 'They've got bloody persil on the menu.'

'Persil is French for Parsley, you know, parsley and thyme which you like in your stuffing.'

'Oh well, that's all right then, but bloody funny it's got

183

the same name as a washing powder ain't it.'

'Well what do you suggest I have Mark, you know what I like.'

'Here dad, have this' responded his son pointing out an item on the menu.

'What's that then son'?

'Well its strips of beef served with jacket potatoes and a range of French vegetables.'

'No funny sauces or anything like that?'

'No dad.'

'Okay then, that sounds fairly safe I will go for that. What are you having?'

'Oh I am having mussels and Maria's going to have trout with almonds.'

'Yuk' replied Sid. 'Is that for your main course a few mussels and almonds with your trout, you need a bit of batter and chips for a real fish meal.'

'Mark duly ordered the meal and they all had a glass of Kir as an aperitif, a pre dinner tipple Sid had become accustomed to and liked.

Sid's was the first meal, or at least plate to appear. It was one of the largest dinner plates Sid had ever seen and on it was a large jacket potato and some green salad. Next to the plate was placed a large serving dish containing peas, green beans and what Sid thought at first glace was mashed swede.

The waitress then disappeared and returned soon afterwards with a trolley on which was a large plate containing thinly cut slices of prime, raw beef which she places beside Sid and along side it what looked to Sid like a small marble chess board about an inch thick inset into a shallow wooden box. Then with a bon appetite the waitress walked briskly away from the table whilst Sid just sat and stared first at his plate then at the beef and the piece of marble.

Meanwhile, on the other side of the table, Maria and Mark were tucking into their meal smiling to themselves.

'Hey Mark' enquired Sid. 'Don't they bloody cook beef over here? I know that they have it fairly rare but this ones not just flipping rare it sodding unique.'

Sid's face was a picture, but Maria couldn't leave him in the state he was in.

'Look dad take your salt cellar and sprinkle it onto that marble slab and be careful not to touch its surface okay.'

'Put salt on that bit of stone, ok if you say so.'

As Sid raised his hand above the stone he suddenly felt heat rising from it.

'Right dad, now take a piece of the beef with your fork and lay it on the block.'

Again Sid did as he was bid and immediately the flesh sizzled.

'Well bugger me' said Sid, 'It's cooking itself, like an indoor barbeque ain't it'

'Yes dad, now all you have to do is cook the meat to your own preference and keep putting new pieces on as you go.

Sid did not need a second telling he was off like a greyhound out of the trap, downing his vegetables and enjoying the French beef.

Meanwhile Maria and Mark continued with their meal

occasionally glancing across at Sid who was experimenting with different areas of the stone and with varying degrees of meat being exposed to the heated surface. By the end of the meal Sid gave it a satisfactory rating of 9 out of 10 (Ten was reserved for his memory of his late wife's cooking) and the trio returned to the cottage well fed and watered with a resignation that they were returning home the next day.

The house was all battened down, water and electricity turned off as the family bode farewell to the dwelling for a few more weeks. Sid had enjoyed his stay in France and whilst he thought he had worked hard both in the house and the garden he also acknowledged that he had been well looked after, fed and watered and experienced things he would never have done back in Creekleigh. As they were passing the village church Sid suddenly asked Mark to stop the car.

'What have you forgotten now dad?'

'Nothing son, its just that I wanted to take a photo of the house over there, the one where I became Mr Shifter or should I say Monsieur Shifter for an afternoon.'

Sid got out of the car and pointed his battered instamatic camera at the group of cottages beyond the church. He then returned to the vehicle and within ten minutes had fallen asleep his head tilted back and snoring so loudly it out performed the sound coming from the Skoda's diesel engine.

Chapter 22

Back home in Creekleigh Sid walked in through his front door and over an assortment of envelopes, leaflets and free newspapers that had been put through his letterbox in the last seven days.

'Home again Fluff' he said as he felt the familiar rubbing of his cat against the side of his leg. 'Has old Mrs Batty been feeding you well since I've been away?' There was no reply from the cat.

Sid sat in his favourite armchair and, with the wastepaper bin next to him began to open the post that had accumulated in his absence.

He had already put the menu from the Peking Pagoda into the receptacle. This was followed by two double-glazing promotion leaflets and an invitation to join Weight Watchers for a special introductory price.

The envelopes contained similar advertising material, but then Sid found one that had been franked by the local district council. Hello, hello thought Sid what do they want now? I bet its more money for something.

On opening the correspondence Sid could see from the

letter heading that it was from the Council's Planning Department and advised Sid that under the councils general procedures to keep local residents fully advised of all issues likely to affect them they were informing him of the submission of a recent planning application. The letter continued by advising that an application had been made by a Mr Ranjeev Patel for a change of use of a shop at No 37 The Avenue to a restaurant with take-a-way facilitates.

What! exclaimed Sid. That must be old Jacobson's place on the corner. He's been there donkey's years. I can recall his father mending my old dad's boots. Always does a good job, but never ready on time. Whenever you go in to collect any repairs he would always respond, 'Ready next Wednesday'. It's a wonder he ever got any repeat business but he was cheap and when he did eventually do a repair it was always a good job. I suppose the old boy's retiring. He must be about 10 years younger than me I would guess. Never married. I suppose he was never ready.

Sid smiled to himself and then glancing down realised why he had suddenly begun to reminisce, a habit he was frequently prone to do. He scanned the letter from the council that advised that he had fourteen days in which to make written representation to them from the date of the letter. Sid looked at the letter which had obviously arrived very soon after he had gone on holiday as he only had a week left in which to let the council know what he thought of the proposals. Usually he had plenty.

How can they allow a restaurant and a take-a-way on that corner mused Sid. There is nowhere to park and there will be bloody chaos in the evenings with people parking on the roadside and blocking traffic. The town centre's the proper location for places to eat not next to people's homes. The place is sure to generate more bloody litter. I suppose with a name like Patel the restaurant will be an Indian and so the smells will be of curry and spices. 'YUK'

Well I certainly intend to make my objection to the proposal thought Sid and I will also make my views known to old Jacobson as well.

The next morning Sid walked the short journey along The Avenue to No 37 and entered the "Creekleigh Cobblers". A bell tingled as the door opened at the sound of which a small grey haired man wearing a leather apron looked up from his last.

'Morning Sidney' he exclaimed as he saw the familiar features through the gloom of the poorly lit shop.

The smell of leather mingled with the adhesive and polish was evocative to Sid and brought back memories of his childhood when all of his shoes were repaired.

'Your shoes will be ready next Wednesday Sid.'

'No they wont you silly bugger, you haven't got any of my shoes at the moment.'

'Oh, I could have sworn you brought a pair of brogues in last week. Anyway, what can I do for you then?'

'I want to know what you are up to Stan. I've just opened a letter from the council advising me that there is a planning application to turn your old shop into an Indian Restaurant.'

'You are not the first person Sid, to come in here and question me on this. Since the planning application went in my bell has never been tinkling so much with people I haven't seen for years coming in to talk to me and bring me their shoes. Best advert I have ever had.'

'Look', Stan pointed to the racks behind him, which

normally had up to half a dozen pairs of shoes on it at any one time. Currently Sid estimated that there were 20 to 30 pairs.

'Well you have obviously got plenty of work Stan so why the change of use?'

'I'm not getting any younger Sid, and quite frankly, until the recent interest in me and the restaurant proposal, business has been very slow and so when Mr Patel made me an offer I thought it was too good an opportunity to miss. But it's all subject to him getting planning permission for his restaurant. If the application fails then so does our agreement. Between you and me Sid I need the money and I wouldn't get the same deal if I sold the premises as a shop. I hope you are not going to object are you.' asked Stan looking over the top of his horn rimmed spectacles and scanning Sid's face for a sign of his intentions.

'Well Stan, I have to admit that the idea of having an Indian restaurant within throwing distance of my house fills me with apprehension. I don't want to spoil our friendship but I am sure you can appreciate my situation. Would you want an Indian Restaurant near your house and everything that it brings with it?'

'Well you must do what you think best Sid but I know that the deal I have with Mr Patel will make all the difference to me in my retirement. The last few years have not been very kind to me Sid with the new heel bar in the town centre taking a lot of my trade. I have got a few debts mounting up and so the offer currently on the table is worth an awful lot to me.'

'Oh I see' said Sid 'Well I had better think about it then.'

'I would be most grateful. From what I have heard there

is a groundswell of local opposition to the proposal and, in particular, the take-a-way and so any support would be most appreciated.'

At that point Sid considered that there was nothing more to be gained or learned from his continued discussion with Stan and so he bade him farewell and promised his old friend that he would think about what they had discussed and that, despite the timetable, he would not be rushed into a decision.

As Sid walked the short distance back to his bungalow he thought about what Stan had said to him and clearly it was important to him that he sold up to Mr Patel as there was an obvious financial incentive. Sid was normally a resolute person and was not easily swayed once he had made a decision but his conversation with Stan had led him to reconsider his position. This indecision, however, did not last for long as he opened his garden gate. There in his flowerbed were two take-a-way polystyrene cartons and a part eaten burger bun.

That's it thought Sid what the hell will my garden be like if we have a take-a-way on the corner of the street. I might as well put up a sign now saying 'Please dump your cartons here.'

Sid did not appreciate the concept of an Indian take-a-way that was normally consumed in the home. He related it to burger bars and fish n chip shops where people ate as they walked along and deposited the relevant packaging as they completed each wrapped or contained item.

Right, where is me writing paper and biro he muttered to himself as he placed the lid on his dustbin and opened his front door.

Sid sat staring at the blank piece of paper in front of him and then at the letter from the council. I wish I was better educated he thought. There are so many things I want to say but don't know how to put them down in writing.

After half an hour Sid had written the date and the words 'Dear Sir, I wish to object…..'

'This is no bloody good is it Fluff' exclaimed Sid as he waved the piece of blue Basildon Bond notepaper at the cat. Fluff fixed him with the blank stare that cats are particularly good at.

'I know I'll go up the Citizens, they are there to help old duffers like me. Perhaps if I tell them the gist of my objections they can make a coherent letter out of it 'cos buggered if I can.'

It had been a little while since Sid had been to the local CAB offices but he noted that the place was looking decidedly shabby and in the case of the external appearance in need of painting and a couple of new window frames.

Inside the waiting room was neat but again the décor was showing signs of distress and the carpet was threadbare by the entrance and the reception area.

There was one other client, as the users of the Citizens Advice Service are now called, sitting with her head bowed reading a copy of Cosmopolitan magazine as Sid introduced himself to the receptionist and asked if he could possibly see an advisor. He was told that they were short staffed that afternoon and that depending on the complexity of the matters they were currently dealing with it could be a wait of anything from twenty to forty-five minutes.

Sid said that he didn't have any other plans for the afternoon and was happy to wait.

'Oh by the way' he asked as he was about to walk away from the desk 'I couldn't help but notice the place seems to be in need of a bit of maintenance its not in such good nick as I last remember it'

'No sir, you're quite right it's a bit of an embarrassment really but we just don't have the funds at the moment. As you know we depend on donations and grants and unfortunately our biggest grant has just been severely cut.' 'Ah government cuts again is it?'

'No sir, historically Creekleigh District Council have provided the largest single grant but this year they have cut this dramatically and so spending on maintenance has been one of the areas we have had to subsequently cut our spending on.'

'Have you been to their offices recently' ask Sid 'They don't appear to be tightening their belt in terms of maintenance. Thick carpets on the floor, flash reception areas and people like you have to work in less than satisfactory conditions. It just don't seem right.'

'I couldn't possibly comment on what you have said sir,' replied the receptionist, 'but we are certainly experiencing hard times.'

At that she turned to her computer monitor and Sid started to walk towards the seating area of the reception. It was then that Sid suddenly realised that the other occupant of the waiting room was his old friend Ethel. A combination of the light shining through the window directly into his eyes and the lowered head reading the magazine had shielded her identity to Sid as he had entered the room.

'Hello Sid, how are you, I half expected you to pop up

and see me following our little chat we had a few weeks back.'

'I was intending to Ethel but what with me going away at Easter and people still asking me to do little jobs and gardening for them, well I just haven't had the time. Sorry'

'That's okay, how have you been keeping?'

'Steady' replied Sid, which was one of his pet responses to anyone asking after his health.

'And you?'

'Well my legs don't get any better and that's why I am up here today. I've got some incapacity benefit forms to complete and quite honestly Sid someone who likes to use four words when one will do must have written them. I started trying to fill it in but I got so confused I thought that the kind people up here would help me.'

'Yah, they are very obliging people.'

'I don't want to put the wrong information down in case I find I am claiming for something I am not entitled to.'

'I know what you mean Ethel. I've had the same situation with me rent rebate.'

Sid then thought for a moment and asked. 'Couldn't your daughter have helped with the forms, seems like a fairly learned girl.'

'Well I am sure she could but she's found herself a new fellah who she appears besotted with. They are always out together I only seem to see her for mealtimes now.'

'Ah, young love aye. Do you remember it Ethel?'

Ethel smiled and went a little red in the face.

Many years ago she and Sid had dated a couple of times but due to a culmination of events, mostly related to Ethel's shyness and an episode in the back row of the Regent Cinema, the potential romance had lasted only a short time.

'So what brings you to the Citizens Sid?'

'Well, you might not be aware, living where you do at the posh end of town.'

Ethel smiled

'But they are planning to put an Indian Restaurant and take-a-way as a replacement for old Jacobson's shop at the corner of my road.'

'No' gasped Ethel in surprise

'I thought they would have to carry Stan out of his shop in a box.'

'Well it seems that he has got a few financial problems and that, combined with his age and the competition from that new place in the High Street and this offer from some Indian chap, he feels his best option is to sell up now.'

'So why does old Stan's proposals bring you up to this place?'

'It seems under planning law that you need the local council's permission to change the use of a shop to a place to eat. At least that's my understanding of it. They sent me a letter telling me about the proposal and that I had fourteen days to make representation in writing.'

'Well if Old Stan needs the money then I suppose that it would be a nice thing to write to the Council telling them that you think they should give him permission for that Indian chap to make his place into a restaurant.'

'Be nice!' exclaimed Sid. 'Be nice. I've come up here to get them to help me write a letter of objection.'

'Why would you want to object Sid? It would upset Stan I am sure.'

'What is being proposed is upsetting me,' responded Sid raising his voice to a level, which got a disapproving frown from both Ethel and the receptionist.

'Sorry' murmured Sid. 'But you don't understand Ethel' he continued in a more conciliatory tone. 'This ain't going to be like the Cozy Café off the High Street. This will be open until god knows when at night with people arriving by car, slamming doors and causing parking problems. Then there is the smell. I don't like foreign food and the thought of me sitting in my garden on a summer's evening with the smell of curry wafting in the breeze is not my idea of fun.'

'Oh, I hadn't realised Sid. Now I can see why you're a bit upset, but you still have to weigh up other people's needs and feelings.'

At that moment one of the doors off the waiting room opened and Ethel was called in to meet her advisor. Sid helped her out of the chair. They exchanged smiles and as she departed Ethel whispered.

'Do what you thinks best Sid, you usually do.'

The door closed behind her and Sid was left as the solitary figure in the waiting room. He had only just started reading about winter digging techniques in a two-year-old copy of Gardeners' World when he too was informed that an advisor had now become available.

 Sid was shown into a small room with a large table and a number of chairs surrounding it. The woman introduced herself as Joyce and after ensuring that Sid was comfortable asked how she could be of assistance.

Sid produced the letter from the council and explained that he wished to object to the proposal but felt unable to express his thoughts and worries in a letter and hoped that the CAB could assist him in the matter. Joyce nodded and after reading the planning notice took up her pen and writing pad and asked Sid to set out his case. This Sid duly did and the advisor listened intently to Sid's thoughts on parking, doors slamming, traffic congestion, smells, general disturbance and litter and made notes as the objections flowed from Sid's lips.

Based on this information Joyce produced a relatively short but concise letter addressed to the council, which she gave to Sid to proof read.

He read it through slowly and at the end expressed his satisfaction and said that it contained all the points he wanted to get across except it did not have the strong language which he would have liked to include but accepted that, in this instance, it might be counter productive. He signed the letter, Joyce photocopied it for her files and he left the premises after inserting 50p into the donation tin, as was his normal practice.

As he was just reaching the street door Sid heard a commotion behind him. Turning round he was just in time to witness two women physically grappling with one another and swearing profusely as they tried to pull each other's hair and thrust their respective bodies in an attempt to wrestle their adversary to the ground.

'Stop it, stop it ' shouted the receptionist as the various doors of the interview rooms around the reception area opened and curious advisors emerged and tried to separate the two women.

Sid looked on in amazement and with not a small degree of interest and amusement. Both women were calling each other bitches, and from the small snippets of vocabulary Sid could understand, the argument appeared to relate to a man called Ian.

Eventually sheer weight of numbers prevailed and four CAB advisors managed to separate the feuding duo who, although standing apart, were spitting and aiming kicks at one another. A smartly dressed small woman of around 50 then addressed the two women in an almost headmistress like manner and told them bluntly that their behaviour had been intolerable and that unless they both left the premises forthwith the police would be called.

At this the larger of the two protagonists let out one more salvo of abuse, wrenched herself free from the man and woman who had been restraining her and stormed out past Sid, almost knocking him over, into the street beyond.

With her departure the demeanour of the other woman changed, she looked around the room at the assembled company and muttered, whilst looking towards the floor, that she was very sorry and deeply embarrassed. She then straightened her skirt, brushed herself down and was about to leave when she suddenly burst into tears and stood sobbing uncontrollably as the two advisors who had moments ago been physically restraining her, turned comforters and confidants.

'He's my husband, I love him, she can't do that, and she must not be allowed...' the sentence tailed off as the sobbing drowned out her words.

The wretched woman was taken into one of the

consulting rooms whilst the woman, who had issued the ultimatum earlier, instructed everyone to return to their duties. Sid, realising that there was no more to be gained from hanging around the offices, opened the front door and walked into the car park. As he turned the corner of the building the woman who had left the feud a few minutes earlier confronted him.

'I suppose she turned on the waterworks as soon as I left' demanded the woman as she spoke directly into Sid's face.

'Well, err, yes she did cry, sobbed 'err heart out actually.'

'Always was a clever cow she was. Her husband left her over a year ago coz she was drinking away all his money and the kids were having to go without. Now he's getting a divorce she is trying to bleed him dry and I ain't going to stand back and let her do it.'

Sid stood staring at the woman. He had little option as she was barring his path and standing so close that he could feel her breathe on his face.

He did not know how to react, whether to agree with her, ignore her, but certainly not, he thought, disagree with her given her obvious state of mind and the possible reaction he might receive if he did. He then suddenly realised that he recognised the woman as being the same person who he had last seen hurling a brick through his neighbour's window. Regrouping his thoughts he listened to the woman's continued rantings.

'I had gone up the Citizens this afternoon to get some advice for Ian as he works long hours and can't easily get here. I saw the cow come out of a room and I just saw red and flew at her. I can tell you I am not proud of what I just did and Ian will be horrified but I am glad I did, it might make that bitch think just a bit more before she gets someone to write the next demanding letter to my Ian.'

At that the woman thanked Sid for confirming what had transpired in the building after she had left and then turned and clattered off in her high heeled shoes in the direction of the town centre leaving him thinking why me, I ain't no agony aunt besides it looks to me as if Ian is stuck between a rock and a hard place. And they call women the weaker sex!

Given the close proximity of the CAB to the council offices Sid decided there and then to take the letter he had just had prepared by Joyce straight round to the Planning Office.

At the reception desk Sid handed the letter over to the harassed occupant of the chair behind the counter who was trying to advise a member of the public that all of the planning officers were either out on site or engaged and so could not spare any time at present to discuss the siting of a neighbours fence.

'Well something needs to be done,' demanded the complainant, 'I pay my rates and if I don't pay them on time then I soon get a snotty letter from your council demanding payment within so many days or else. Well I think that I should have the same rights, he who pays the piper calls the tune.'

Sid stood back and smiled, go on my son he thought to himself, you keep at it and the girl will eventually weaken and she will get someone in a suit off his arse from upstairs to come down to see you. I've done it myself. The one sided debate between the aggrieved resident and the besieged receptionist continued for a few more minutes before she agreed that she would try again to get someone to talk to the man who she addressed as Mr Beckwith.

She picked up the receiver of the telephone on her desk, tapped out a few numbers and then in a low tone, inaudible to Sid, or Mr Beckwith, spoke to the unfortunate planning officer who had picked up the telephone upstairs.

After a very brief conversation she put the receiver down.

'Sorry sir, but as you can see from the notice here,' she pointed to a printed sheet on the wall adjacent to her desk,

"Please Note that a duty planning officer will be available for consultation daily between 9:30 and 11:30. At all other times an appointment will be necessary"

Oh, thought Sid, the old trick of trying to wear down the receptionist didn't work this time.

'So' exclaimed the complainant 'I either have to make an appointment or come back here again tomorrow morning and get in a queue to see one of your officers for something that should only take about 5 minutes.'

'I am afraid so sir' came the response.

'It's worse than the bloody doctor's this place' fumed the man with the problem. 'Well listen here young lady, I can see you have tried to get someone to help but may I suggest that you tell your colleagues on the first floor that we the public cannot drop everything and turn up in a two hour window. This fence didn't go up until lunchtime today and it's right on the corner of James Street and Folly Avenue. Anyone now trying to drive out of the Avenue can't see to the right any more coz this bloody fence is too high and right in your line of vision. If there is an accident before your council takes any action, then I will make sure that the appropriate people know of your council's tardiness. Yes that's right put it in your book and I will be back tomorrow.'

Sid followed Mr Beckwith out of the offices and watched him get into a rusting Toyota and with a cloud of fumes from his exhaust he sped away. Need a few more of him and me around thought Sid, keep the council on their toes.

Chapter 23

The evening of the planning committee Sid decided that he should go along and see just what was going to be decided about old Stan's shop and, out of curiosity more than anything else, how his beloved councillors made decisions on planning matters. Sid had never been to a council planning meeting before but assumed it would be just like any other council meeting with the ruling Conservative party steam rolling through whatever the party leader and his henchmen had decided was best for the town, or more likely, themselves.

As was his custom Sid arrived at the council offices well in advance of the scheduled 8:00 start time and on entering the council chamber he was asked to sign in and was given a copy of the Agenda for the evening's proceedings. Sid estimated that it contained twenty–five to thirty pages and not being one of the world's greatest readers he immediately sought assistance from a dark suited man who was scurrying up and down at the head of the room with bundles of files and rolls of what Sid later found out were drawings.

'Excuse me young man' enquired Sid 'Can you help me?'

'I'm rather busy at the moment sir,' replied the anxious individual, 'I am trying to prepare the presentation for tonight and I am running short of time'

'Sorry' replied Sid 'I only wanted to know if someone could tell me when you are going to talk about old Stan's place,'

'I am sorry sir' replied the officer, who now he was closer, Sid had identified from his security badge that he was Chris Searle, area Planning Officer.

'I can't tell you off hand, it should be clear from the Agenda which I see you have a copy of in your hand.'

'I know I have an Agenda but I can't make head nor tail of it. It's full of long reference numbers and things called conditions.'

Chris Searle but down his laptop and walked round the top table.

'Now sir, do you know the address or what the proposal is for?'

'Old, I mean Stan Jacobson's application. It's the one for the change of use from the cobblers into an Indian restaurant.'

'Ah yes sir, it's an application by a Mr Patel. As far as I can recall its number 10 on the agenda.'

'Number 10' responded Sid, 'how long will it take to get to that?'

'Oh you can never be sure sir, it depends how long the councillors take to debate those before it but I would guess a couple of hours.'

'Cor, it's worse than the waiting at the doctors for your

number to come up ain't it.'

Chris Searle smiled. 'Now sir, if you are okay I must get on and get my Power Point sorted out.'

'Yeah sure' replied Sid, not having the slightest idea what a power point was.

With about 10 minutes to the start of the proceedings the council chamber was beginning to fill up with a number of local residents, some of whom Sid knew, sitting in the public gallery. By this time Sid had thumbed his way through the green pages of the agenda and found the item relating to the proposed restaurant.

On reading through it he had deduced that the Council were not going to approve the application as the document stated that the proposal should be refused on traffic, parking and local amenity grounds. Following this there was a long list of Policy numbers and comments that it was contrary to this and that. Good, thought Sid, they appear, for a change, to have read what I sent to them and agreed with me. Regardless of this he decided to stay and hear what was going to be said, but as he had been told it might take a couple of hours for the item to come up he ought to go and find the gents.

On exiting the Chamber Sid was confronted with a long corridor to both his left and right but thankfully for him there was a large yellow arrow pointing to the right under which were the letters WC. Sid walked past a number of large imposing panelled doors with the words 'Leader of the Council' and 'Deputy Mayor' on brass plates until he came to his destination.

On entering Sid found himself standing next to two men, both very smartly dressed. They had been talking as Sid entered the room but had stopped abruptly as they realised that they were no longer alone. They however ignored Sid's presence and washed their hands in silence.

The older man was probably in his early sixties and was vaguely familiar to him but he could not recall from where. The other man was younger and Sid thought he was either Indian or Pakistani. The two men had both clearly been talking about that evening's proceedings because as Sid had entered the room he had heard them saying that the planning application would be a formality. The two suited men turned and left the gents still choosing to ignore Sid's presence who, standing by the hand dryer was still trying to recall from where he knew the older white man.

As Sid walked back along the corridor to the Council chamber he noted that just to the other side of the main door was a photomontage of all the district councillors and their chief officers. A right rogues gallery if ever there was one thought Sid as his eyes scanned the various faces staring out at him.

'Hello, hello' he suddenly exclaimed. There he is, I knew I recognised the face. He was Bill Hollingsworth, known as Bill the Builder amongst other less respectable names, and beneath his photograph was the title Leader of the Council. He's always in the local paper for some reason or another and got his fingers in so many pies it's a wonder he ever gets time to build anything. I wonder what he was discussing then in the gents, some building scam I bet. Oh well better get back into the council chamber and see what is happening.

By the time Sid had got back into the room the proceedings were about to begin and he found it difficult finding a spare seat in the public gallery that was by now almost filled to capacity. Sid located a seat towards the back and sat down next to a small grey haired lady with a note book and pen clutched in her hand and a large flat briefcase from which she was extricating a number of typed sheets of paper. On the other side of Sid was a young man, in his twenties he guessed, dressed in blue jeans and a red sweatshirt with the words Manchester United – Red Devils emblazoned on it. Another sad supporter a long way from home smiled Sid.

The young man appeared quite agitated Sid thought and was continually thumbing through his copy of the agenda and underlining parts with a green felt tipped pen. As the meeting commenced Sid turned to look towards the councillors in the chamber and immediately noted that Bill Hollingsworth was sitting centre stage and that to his right was another man who Sid knew well, Councillor Digby the owner of a local timber yard and builders merchants and a cohort of the council leader.

Sid continued to scan the room and then suddenly realised that sitting right in front of him was old Jacobson and next to him was the Indian bloke he had seen talking to the councillor in the gents earlier. The two men were whispering and smiling at one another. Don't know what Jacobson's got to smile about thought Sid, ain't he read the agenda, the proposal to convert his place to a restaurant is set to be thrown out and with it his big payday.

Then suddenly it began to dawn on Sid that the Indian chap must be Mr Patel who was intending to buy the cobblers and change it into an Indian Takeaway. So what was he doing talking to Bill Hollingsworth earlier?

As he mused on this his attention was drawn to the proceedings, from which he decided that Councillor Digby was the Chairman of the Planning Committee, and that by the way he was conducting proceedings he was going to have an important if not fundamental input into that evenings decisions.

Slowly the various applications were introduced by the chairman and following a brief explanation of a sites history and a description of the proposal there was very little debate and so the officer's recommendations for approval or refusal were virtually agreed almost unopposed. That was until item number seven on the agenda was introduced. It was clear to Sid from the activity and interest suddenly being given to the proceedings from the Manchester United supporter next to him that this particular application was the reason for his attendance that evening.

Item number seven announced Councillor Digby is in relation to the use of the property known as 'Smallwood' at Creekleigh Road for the selling and distribution of flowers, plants and vegetables. Ah thought Sid, I know that place. It's a little bungalow on the edge of town near the doctor's house, got a good plot of land around it and a couple of greenhouses as I recall. Yeah, I remember the doctor telling me he bought some of his cacti from there.

Chris Searle explained to the assembly that the selling of goods from the premises had been going on for the last eighteen months without the benefit of planning permission and that the council had served an enforcement notice on the owner and trader, a Mr Smythe, to cease trading. The committee was informed that the offender had failed to do so but had as he was entitled, made a retrospective planning application to regularise the situation. The planning officer then set out the history of the council's involvement over the last year and a half and confirmed that the council officers were now content that with the provision of off-road parking and, subject to the site being limited to the sale of what was produced on the premises, that planning consent should be granted.

However, as the debate ensued it became clear that this was one application that was not going to entirely follow an officer's recommendation.

Committee members of the controlling Conservative Party were clearly determined to make a case for the refusal of the application and introduced a number of issues. These included claims that the road near the site was an accident black spot and that the extra traffic it generated would create noise and disturbance to neighbours, albeit no neighbours had objected and in fact one had written to the council in support of the proposals. Eventually the discussion came to an end and a vote was taken. As the hands went up Sid looked to his right to see the anxious look on the face of the young man next to him.

Councillor Digby counted the raised hands and announced that the development had failed to find favour with the committee and so should be refused on grounds of highway safety and local amenity.

During these proceedings Sid had been conscious that the man next to him had become extremely agitated and as the decision was announced Sid turned to look at him and saw his face was almost as crimson as his sweatshirt.

'You bastards' he shouted, at which point the whole assembly turned to look at him.

'You absolute two-faced bastards' he repeated.

Couldn't have put it better myself thought Sid.

The chairman banged his gavel and requested order, but

the young man was too incensed to heed his request. He got up from his seat and walked out of the chamber but not before standing in the doorway and shouting that 'The whole council was morally bankrupt and devoid of any sense of integrity and that he would get professional advice and maybe appeal the application.'

Eventually the hubbub died down in the council chamber, order was restored and item number 8 on the agenda was introduced. This, along with number 9 both related to relatively small domestic applications entailing extension works and were, after very limited debate nodded through.

Item number ten was then introduced. "The proposed redevelopment of No.37 The Avenue to create a restaurant and take-a-way facility."

Once again the hard working planning officer set out the background to the proposal and explained that the development was contrary to the local plan insofar as it was deemed to create problems in terms of traffic, parking and local amenity. Chris Searle also advised that there had been a lot of public interest in the proposal to the extent the Council had received a total of 21 letters of representation of which twelve were in favour and nine against.

At this point Jacobson turned around in his seat and stared into Sid's eyes. Nothing was said but Sid felt distinctly uncomfortable as he realised that the cobbler knew that one of the letters of objection had emanated from him and he felt let down and slighted by this fact. After what seemed like an age to Sid, the aggrieved man again turned his back on Sid both physically and metaphorically.

Sid thought to himself, I only did what I thought was right and besides the council are going to throw the proposal out anyway so my little intervention shouldn't be considered in any way instrumental in old Jacobson loosing his big payday from Mr Patel. However, Sid soon realised that the refusal of the restaurant proposal was by no means a formality as one councillor after another began to speak in glowing terms of the need for a new ethnic restaurant in the town and how the site of the cobblers lent itself to such a facility.

It was then for the first time that evening that Bill Hollingsworth spoke and advocated that despite the council's agreed policy the proposed restaurant could be considered a much needed addition to the towns eating establishments and that car parking was not an issue as most patrons would walk to and from it. Walk; thought Sid, the people of this town have forgotten what their legs are for. Virtually all the kids are driven to and from school in bloody great cars big enough to accommodate four or five but normally there is only one.

Everyone drives to the supermarket, in my day you had no choice there was walk, cycle, or stay put and wait for one of the delivery vans to call. No kid went to school by car. They all walked, cycled, or those from the outlying villages came by school bus.

However, the pro development stance taken by the leader of the council was echoed by a number of his colleagues of the same political persuasion, whilst the minority parties agreed with the planning officer that the development should be refused.

During the debate Sid listened intently and at the same time observed the two figures in front of him. They both seemed relatively relaxed as if they knew that the result would go their way and so once a vote was finally taken at the end of the debate the majority party and Bill Hollingsworth won the day with the voting going along party lines.

At this announcement Jacobson stretched out his hand to Mr Patel and with a broad smile on their faces shook hands warmly.

What a bloody carves up thought Sid and how these councillors can be so two-faced. That poor bloke next to me gets refused coz they claim that traffic will cause problems, but the restaurant gets the thumbs up.

'The whole thing smells to me' exclaimed Sid in a low voice. 'There is something not quite right about all this' and he was right.

Item ten had turned out to be last item on the agenda with eleven having been withdrawn at the applicant's request earlier in the day. So as Sid rose from his seat he could see Jacobson and the prospective purchaser of his shop talking to a group of councillors, but as he turned he found his exit was obstructed by the little grey haired lady who was trying to collect her various bits of stationery together and only succeeding in dropping her pencils under the seat in front.

As Sid bent down to help her she quietly whispered to him

'I overheard you talking to yourself at the end of the meeting. I do apologise but if it is not too impertinent to ask what did you mean by it being a carve up'

'Oh' exclaimed Sid 'I didn't know anyone was listening, its just an old man musing on what he has seen and his jaundiced view of our councillors. I don't suppose there has been any wrong doing and I am old enough to know that the world is not a fair or equitable place but sometimes it does make you wonder?'

Sid was about to ask the woman why she had any interest in his thoughts when he caught sight of a badge pinned to her cardigan, which read "PRESS".

'You from the local paper' enquired Sid suddenly realising that a fellow member of the local community was not questioning him out of idle curiosity.

'Yes, I am Elizabeth Taylor, 'and before you ask no I have not had a string of husbands, in fact I am single and always have been.'

'Okay' replied Sid suddenly taken aback by the feistiness of what until now he had considered was a diminutive grey haired lady in her late fifties.

'I know that name, aren't you the woman at the paper who wrote about the contracts that the councils were handing out as part of their privatisation of services.'

'Yes.'

'And wasn't it a result of your digging around that a couple of officers resigned from the council over something to do with building contracts and a councillor was also implicated, I recall, but he has managed to keep his position.'

'Quite right Mr err…'

'Saines, Sid Saines'

'Well Sid, if I may call you that, like you I also do not trust this council and I believe that this stinks, excuse the expression, and what I uncovered in relation to the supply of materials and contract for building the new toilets was just the tip of the iceberg. The scandal and implications go far deeper and higher into the council than just the two middle ranking officers that took the can for the Potter Street public convenience debacle.

'Its clear to me Sid, that between us, we may be able to take my crusade to another level. You clearly know more than you are letting on and I have a number of contacts within the council who are becoming very agitated, and whilst fearing for their jobs are, if confronted with some well resourced facts, likely to spill the beans. Sid was intrigued and also slightly worried as to what he might be getting into but the reporter seemed charged with a resolve to get at the truth from the council she clearly distrusted and with Sid's long time distain for their operations and "them and us culture" he felt that he should at least investigate what Elizabeth was trying to achieve and so he agreed to meet her in her office the next morning.

Chapter 24

That evening Sid sat in his favourite armchair sucking his pipe of Old Holborn and, whilst stroking Fluff, considered the events of the Council meeting and in particular the interlude in the gents toilets and the apparent relationship between Mr Patel, Jacobson and Bill Hollingsworth.

I'm bloody sure they were in cahoots over old Jacobson proposals Fluff, don't you think the whole thing stinks?'

Fluff looked up at the mention of his name but the only thing that stank to him was the odour coming from Sid's pipe and the smell of burning bread from the kitchen where his master had forgotten that he had put some bread under the grill to toast!

Sid rose the next morning as soon as his alarm sounded at 7:30.

As a creature of habit he went to the kitchen, put on the kettle and fed Fluff who made his presence felt by constantly rubbing round Sid's legs until he retrieved the can opener from the cutlery drawer and opened the tin of Kit-e-Kat. At that point Fluff's affections for Sid evaporated as he turned his attention to devouring the mixture of meat and jelly in his bowl. For his part Sid went into the bathroom for a wash and a shave whilst his tea was brewing in the brown china teapot sitting on the kitchen work surface.

Following a breakfast of tea and toast eaten in his pyjamas and dressing gown Sid dressed in readiness for his meeting that morning with Elizabeth Taylor of the Creekleigh Gazette.

His appointment was for nine fifteen but Sid found himself standing outside the paper's offices in the High Street as the town clock struck nine. To while away the next ten minutes or so Sid studied the photographs in the window of the office. These consisted of pictures from the current edition of the paper and were of a similar kind to those found in numerous local newspaper offices the length and breadth of the country.

There was one that particularly intrigued Sid, as it was an old sepia coloured photograph showing the front of the now demolished Regent Cinema that had formerly stood in the High Street. The photo was one of an occasional series where old photographs of the town were printed and readers invited to write in about their memories and recollections of when it was taken. Sid's mind began to wander back to the 1940s and Sunday afternoons and evenings spent watching films in what had been called the local fleapit. Memories of Ethel, and a few other local girls, came flooding back into his thoughts and foremost amongst these was his wife who he had taken on their first date to the cinema in 1947. He recalled how shy she had been and how he had tried so hard to impress. Must have done something right he thought coz she eventually married me.

Sid was suddenly brought back to reality by a voice saying, 'Hello Mr Saines, I am so please you have come.'

'Oh err yes, well' stammered Sid who for the moment was disorientated by both his thoughts and the uncertainty as to where the voice was coming from.

'Please come in. I will get Sophie to make us some tea and then we can chat in peace and quiet.'

'Thank you' replied Sid gathering his senses and walking through the main door into the office's reception. Sid had been into the reception area a number of times to place the odd advert or purchase a particular photograph but he had never been beyond the public area and was intrigued as to what he might find behind the doors leading away from it.

He was disappointed, as all he could see was a relatively short length of corridor off of which were a number of similar doors with no distinguishing signs and as far as he could observe, or hear, very little activity. Sid had not been sure what he had expected to find but he had envisaged that a newspaper office with its various deadlines would have been a bit livelier than it was at present. Par for the course, I suppose, he thought. Nothing ever happens in this town so why should the newspaper office be any different.

Sid was ushered into a room that had wall-to-wall filing cabinets and in the centre of which was a desk piled high with brown and blue files which almost obscured the computer that sat amongst them. The walls were adorned with old film posters and photographs of actors and actresses from an age that Sid recognised, amongst which was one of Jean Harlow who had been Sid's favourite.

'Now then Mr Saines.'

'Call me Sid.'

'Thank you. Well Sid, have you thought any more about last night's goings on at the Council Committee meeting?'

'To be honest,' replied Sid. 'since we spoke I haven't been able to get it out of my head.'

'Well I am pleased you have been thinking about things Sid and, getting back to last night, can you recall what, if anything, you overheard in the gents.'

'Well, as I recall, as I entered the room Bill was saying to the Indian bloke something like, 'It's in the bag' and 'I have had a chat to some people.' Then I could not quite hear what was said next but he finished up by saying 'and they are with me on this'

'Did Mr Patel say anything?'

'All I heard from him was something like 'good, then we will all benefit.'

After that they realised my presence and did not even have the common courtesy to acknowledge me.'

'It seems from what you overheard Sid that there is some connection with Mr Patel and Bill and I wouldn't mind betting that money, or property or both are at the heart of it.'

'Maybe' responded Sid 'but just because I overheard a bit of a conversation and the council made one of their strange planning decisions don't make this to be some kind of fiddle does it?'

'No, not on its own Sid, but as you just said, the council in recent years has had the habit of making some very strange planning decisions both in approving and rejecting development proposals. In fact, it has got to the situation that they have refused so many against the advice of their planning staff that they are having to appoint external consultants to represent them when these go to appeal as their own staff cannot support their reasons for objection.'

'Oh' replied Sid, not fully comprehending what Elizabeth was saying but realising that she had clearly been gathering information about the inconsistencies of the council and its planning decisions over some time.

'Well that is all very interesting' remarked Sid 'But apart from me adding my three penn'orth about what I witnessed the other night I don't see how much more help I can be. You have clearly been on the case for some time.'

'Ah but you can Sid.   Look, the councillors and the officers at the council know me.'

They know me as well thought Sid; at least they do in the housing department.

'I need some assistance from someone who is clearly of a like mind to myself and distrusts the council, or the councillors at least, and could do a bit of prying without arousing any suspicion.'

'I ain't no James Bond' replied Sid 'and I am afraid that I ain't clever or learned enough to go through loads of papers, and besides I wouldn't know what I was looking at or for.'

'No, no Sid, I appreciate that. What I was hoping to do was persuade you to use your obvious local knowledge and contacts to find out some more background information on specific matters I believe are being used to financially benefit a number of Councillors.'

Sid was still uncertain as to where the conversation was going but he let Elizabeth continue.

'Look Sid, I am pretty sure that I know of at least 4

potential development sites, and I reckon there are considerably more, that have had planning applications manipulated by the ruling councillors. Just take for example the restaurant proposal the other night, we both believe there was some skulduggery going on, but proving it is another matter. You, however, know the owner of the property personally and whilst I am sure he wouldn't tell you that anything underhand had gone on, he might let something slip or give you a clue as to where we might take our enquiries next.'

'Well I don't know about that' replied Sid. 'He knows that I sent a letter of objection to the council about the proposal. He is hardly likely to welcome me back into his shop with the offer of a chat over a cup of tea and a bit of Victoria Sponge Sandwich is he?'

'Well I suppose not, but you see what I am getting at Sid. I can provide you with a bit of background information and all I ask is to see what the odd enquiry here and there brings forth. For example, I am not convinced that there is not something going on at the site of Smallwood off Creekleigh Road.'

'What, do you mean the place of that Manchester United supporter last night?'

'Well yes, if that's what he was.'

'Well he lives hundreds of miles away from Old Trafford so it's quite likely that he does. Why he can't support his local team, Creekleigh Athletic I don't know, but come to think of it perhaps I can. Anyway why do you say that? What have the council to gain in refusing the chap the opportunity to carry on trading apart from their vindictive nature.'

'That decision last night smelt of wrong doing to me and I could see from the planning officer's demeanour that he was far from happy with the decision. Have you considered Sid where the property is?'

'Well' he replied 'Its on one of the main roads out of Creekleigh, good spot I suppose for catering for passing custom and probably still close enough to attract people to go out of the town to buy stuff.'

'Precisely Sid and if you were aware of the council's planning policy you would see that the site sits just outside of the area currently scheduled for development.'

'So what?'

'This makes his land a prime development site for when the council next look at future extensions to the town's boundary and as a result, what is currently agricultural land with agricultural land use values, could soar in price if it becomes designated for industrial or housing development.'

'Be worth a bit then would it' asked Sid.

'Worth a bit! Probably one million pounds an acre.'

'Bloody hell' interjected Sid. 'I didn't know we were talking about this sort of money, I thought we were looking at Old Bill getting to build the odd dodgey house here and there or maybe doing a bit of restoration and renovation.'

'No Sid, we are talking big money, we are talking about manipulation of the planning process and corruption in a big way.'

'So why have the council, or specific member of it decided to refuse planning permission for that bloke's farm shop.'

'I don't know Sid but I am sure it relates to land values.'

221

Sid sat and stared across the room, his gaze fixed on a picture of girls strapped to the wings of an aircraft with the words "FLYING DOWN TO RIO" emblazoned on the bottom of the poster. He was all for trying to get back at the local council, and the councillors in particular, for what he considered were years of doing him down but the figures that Elizabeth was talking about made him distinctly nervous.

The reporter could see from the look of apprehension on Sid's face that her last remark had caused him to reflect on the situation and anxious not to loose the obvious initial enthusiasm of Sid she decided that this was a good point to end the discussion for the morning.

'Well Sid, you can see that I believe we could be into something big here and I would love you to help me but I realise that you must have some reservations. I suggest you go home and think about what we have talked over, but please, do not disclose any of this to anyone else as it is important that we keep mum on this and I am sure I can rely on you.'

'Oh err yes of course, it's just that I did not realise quite what it was you wanted to talk about this morning and frankly I had no idea this sort of thing could be going on in Creekleigh. It's the sort of thing you read about in the News of the World on Sundays not the Creekleigh Gazette on a Thursday.'

At that Elizabeth stood up and stretched out her bejewelled hand to Sid.

'Thanks for coming Sid, I will give you a call in a couple of days and hopefully we can meet again to discuss things in greater detail. Meanwhile, if you have a chance to do a bit of sniffing around feel free.'

'Yeah, okay. As you say, I need to go home and have a long think.'

As Sid stood on the pavement outside of the newspaper offices he glanced down at the advertising board promoting that week's edition of the Gazette. The hand written headline read "COUNCIL TAX RATES SET TO SOAR".

The bastards thought Sid as he walked across the High Street to the sound of a blasting car horn and tinkling of a cycle bell as both driver and cyclist narrowly avoided the preoccupied pensioner.

Back in his bungalow Sid sat in his favourite armchair, sucked on his pipe and considered the morning's events. He was not one of the world's great thinkers and was by nature a spur of the moment character, a philosophy that sometimes got him into trouble as he often reacted or spoke out without thinking about the consequences and then regretted his impatience. An example of this being the confrontation he had had with the customs officer at Dover.

However in this instance Sid was very troubled by the dilemma he found himself in.

He would dearly love to help in any exposing of the council's or councillors' wrong doing but the sheer scale of the potential misdemeanour that had been outlined to him that morning made him uncharacteristically reticent.

Eventually, and after much soul searching, Sid decided that he would grab the bull by the horns and pay a visit to Old Jacobson's place. This was not such a ground breaking decision as he had a pair of shoes to collect which he had left when he had last visited the shop and had not returned, due in part to his action in objecting to the planning application.

Chapter 25

So it was that the next day Sid stood outside the Creekleigh Cobblers and noted the SOLD sign, which was affixed to the site frontage.

Didn't waste much bloody time did he, thought Sid, as he entered the gloomy interior to the sound of the shop bell.

Jacobson looked up and saw the familiar frame of Sid Saines silhouetted in the doorway.

'A fine mate you turned out to be Sid. Just as well the council saw sense and ignored your bloody objection. You knew how important it was to me to get that permission but you still went out of your way to object.'

Sid felt uncomfortable but had been ready for this reaction.

'It's all very well for you to just sell up with a nice little nest egg and bugger off across town. Me and the neighbours are left with the smell litter, traffic and inconvenience of having an Indian Take-a-way on our doorstep.'

'Come on Sid, it wont be as bad as that. Mr Patel assured

me that it would be a good quality establishment with extractor fans and a mission statement to help ensure that it is a good neighbour.'

'Mission Statement' exclaimed Sid. 'How will he be able to control what his customers will do with their containers on a Saturday night, after they have had a few pints in the White Horse. As for the extractor fans all they will do is take the curry smell out his restaurant and blow it all over the homes of the poor buggers that surround it.'

'Well I am sorry you feel that way Sid but, as I said, I felt hurt when I was told that you had raised a formal objection but thanks to the councillors, and Mr Patel and his backers, it's all systems go and I should be out of here within the next couple of weeks. So, if you were thinking of leaving any shoes for repair then you are too late because I am not accepting any more. When these are repaired, he gestured towards about twenty pairs of shoes stacked in a dishevelled heap behind him, that's me finished forever.'

'I ain't brought any shoes with me, I've come to collect a pair.'

'Oh yes, now I remember. I did them yesterday, I did think about refusing to do them but I don't let a grudge get in the way of earning a bit of cash. I got me planning permission despite your best efforts Sid.'

'Yeah, maybe but it was against what the planning officer advised wasn't it.'

'It's not what you know but who you know Sid.'

'So who did you know then' enquired Sid sensing that he might be getting somewhere.

'I ain't saying any more, just that Mr Patel is a very

influential businessman and clearly the council felt that his proposals warranted approval and who am I to disagree.'

'Well he clearly appeared very pally with Bill Hollingsworth.'

'As I said, Ranjeev is well connected. I believe this restaurant will be his third in the district, not counting the other catering enterprises he is involved in. You've probably seen some of the white vans around the town with the Cobra Supplies logo on the side made up in the form of curled snakes. Well he is the major shareholder of that company and sees my premises as helping to further his catering empire. Believe me Sid; I think your fears are unfounded and that the restaurant and take-a-way will be a benefit to the town.'

'As I see it Stan, you may be alright ....' But before he could complete the sentence Sid was interrupted by the cobbler who had clearly had enough of what he considered was his old friend's sniping.

'Look Sid, just accept that the democratic system has decided that, in this instance, I won and you lost. I'm retiring, there will be a new restaurant on this spot and you will have to put up with the consequences. In all developments there has to be winners and losers and for a change I am a winner.'

'Here are your shoes Sid, that will be £7:50 and I have put in a new pair of laces at a nominal charge.'

Sid handed over the money and without a further word turned and walked out of the shop.

Well I am pleased to be out of there thought Sid, it made me feel a bit uneasy but I still think it was selfish on his part insofar as what the proposals will inflict on local residents.

Sid was not sure if his visit had secured any useful information to impart to Elizabeth except for the fact that that Mr Patel appeared to be a more important player than he had first imagined and not simply an Indian attempting to set up an independent restaurant and take-a-way and was, it appeared, an influential business man and restaurateur.

The next morning Sid again visited the Gazette offices and was pleased to find Elizabeth was in and available to talk to him. She inquired if he had come to any conclusion about assisting her in her crusade and was pleased to hear that Sid had already visited the cobbler and was anxious to hear what he had elicited from his conversation.

'Despite his newfound wealth' reported Sid 'he is still as tight as a duck's arse. Repaired me old black shoes and even charged me extra for a new pair of laces that I could have bought cheaper in Woolies.'

Elizabeth smiled. 'That's the businessman in him Sid.'

'I call it tight' replied the man wearing the re-heeled shoes.

'Well did you find out anything we didn't already know Sid' she asked quizzically.

'Not a lot I am afraid. I felt a bit awkward really, and strangely embarrassed, which is not something I normally suffer from particularly with men and people I know.' Clearly, thought Elizabeth, noticing that in his haste to dress that morning he had failed to fix his fly buttons on his trousers.

'I did find out that Jacobson believed that it was through Mr Patel's connections that he had managed to help secure the councils permission and that he owns a number of investments in the district and some form of catering operations known as Cobra Supplies but old Jacobson didn't appear to know much detail about this. It was also clear from me conversation that he and old Bill Hollingsworth are good mates but again he wouldn't say, or did not know, any more than that.'

'This is interesting Sid and gives us another angle, particularly as Hollingsworth is also in the development business. You normally find that fellow developers either work hand in hand or hate each other and in this particular case there appears to be some kind of mutual appreciation going on.'

'Is there anything else I can do to help at the moment' enquired Sid.

'Not at the moment Sid, just keep your ear to the ground, our discussion this morning has given me a further impetus to follow a lead which I had been tentatively considering.'

'Okay' responded Sid who was pleased to know that his embarrassment of the previous day had possibly yielded some useful information.

For the remainder of that week and into the next Sid had no more contact with Elizabeth and for his part Sid had no desire to visit the cobblers and so without further investigations from his mentor he pursued his regular routine of odd-jobbing, gardening, tending his greenhouse and clearing rubbish from his front garden.

However, late on Wednesday evening Sid's telephone rang and, expecting it was a cold call from some call centre on the Indian Sub continent trying to sell him something he had managed to do without for the last 77 years, he barked down the phone.

'Yes, whatever it is I don't want it.'

He was about to hang up when he heard Elizabeth's familiar voice.

'Don't hang up Sid, I have some news for you.'

'Oh sorry Elizabeth, I didn't mean to be rude but this time of the evening the only calls I normally get are from people with foreign accents trying to flog something.'

'First of all may I apologise for not keeping in contact with you but after our chat last week you set a few cogs going in my mind and I think you might be very interested in what has developed in recent days.

I believe Sid you might find that tomorrows copy of the Gazette will be interesting reading for a number of people and uncomfortable for a few others.'

'Do you mean that you have come up with something' asked Sid almost unable to control a tremor of anticipation in his voice.

'Well lets just say that I believe Councillor Bill Hollingsworth will have to consider his position over the next few days and may be your old friend Jacobson will not be retiring quite as soon as he thought. (Anyway Sid, as I said, thanks again and may be in a few days we can get together and I can buy you lunch on behalf of the Gazette.)

'Oh' replied Sid. 'Thank you, but I haven't done much, just spoke to old Jacobson and simply confirmed what he told me to you.'

'I know Sid, but it helped me to explore other avenues of enquiry, as the police say, and as a result I believe we have opened an almighty can of worms. Now then where would you like to go? I assume you don't want Chinese or Indian, so how about The Parisian.'

Sid thought back to his recent holiday in France.

'Well to tell the truth' he said 'I like the Cozy Café.'

'Well that's fine by me Sid, shall we say next Tuesday at twelve. Enjoy your reading tomorrow' and at that she rang off.

Well bugger me thought Sid, what on earth can she have found out that is likely to cause the rumpus she was describing.

The next morning Sid could hardly contain his curiosity. He hastily ate his breakfast and at 7:00, as the local newsagents opened, Sid was standing on the doorstep.

He could see George Greene, who, along with his father Alfred, had run Greene's Newsagents and Tobacconists for over 50 years and as in most shops in the town Sid was no stranger.

'Morning Sid', announced George, a rotund individual of about 50. 'You're early this morning, run out of fag papers again?' Won't be a minute I have just to put this advert out for today's Gazette.'

Sid watched as the newsagent fixed the sheet of paper he was carrying to the advertising hording on the shop frontage. The hand written headline read 'COUNCIL PLANNING PROBE – OMBUDSMAN TO INVESTIGATE'.

'Now then Sid what can I do for you?'

'I'd like a copy of the Gazette please, half an ounce of Old Holborn and yes some red papers please.'

As he handed over his purchases George remarked that

the council appeared to have got them selves into a bit of bother.

'Seems that there has been some underhand work going on and contracts let in exchange for favours. Anyway, I can't talk any longer Sid I've got to get the paper boys out on their rounds, local paper day is always a busy one.'

'Oh yeah, thank you' replied Sid as he walked out of the shop trying to read the front page without his spectacles and narrowly avoiding a collision with a cycle that had been left unattended outside the shop by a paper boy clearly late for his delivery collection.

Sid decided that it would probably be safer to wait until he got home to read the paper and so he hurried off to the comfort of his armchair and with his pipe in one hand and a cup of Camp coffee at his elbow he began to read.

Under the banner headlines of "Ombudsman to Investigate Council Procedure" Sid read that it had been brought to the attention of the Chief Executive, Andrew Snow, that there had been a number of inconsistencies in recent council planning decisions and that amongst these there had emerged a common denominator.

The article went on to say that the Chief Executive had been given a list of a number of recent planning decisions all of which had been determined contrary to advice by the planning officers. Of these, 4 could be related directly, or indirectly, to the operations of a company trading as Cobra Supplies or one of its subsidiaries.

Hang on a minute thought Sid, that's the name Jacobson gave me as being a company owned by Mr Patel.

The report continued by claiming that it had firm evidence that Cobra Supplies and councillors at Creekleigh

District Council had been in collusion over various planning decisions and that in particular Councillor Bill Hollingsworth had gained a pecuniary interest (Sid had to get his Collins Pocket Dictionary out for this word) out of the company's activities and had not declared this when voting in Committee on matters associated with it.

It was also stated by the newspaper that the recently awarded contract for catering supplies at the council, including the running of the new privatised canteen, had been secured through a 'deal between the Chair of the Planning Committee and Cobra Supplies'.

Crikey, thought Sid, Elizabeth has gone to town. I only hope she has got the facts right cos what she is saying appears pretty damn strong to me.

The article concluded with the comment that all of the evidence collected by the Gazette had been forwarded to the police who in a brief statement advised that they were looking into the matter but that at this particular time had no further comments to make.

Beneath the article was a photograph of Bill Hollingsworth who was quoted as saying that the allegations made by the newspaper were spurious and unfounded and that he would defend his good name with every breathe in his body and that the accusations were a slur, not just against him, but his fellow councillors and officers of Creekleigh District Council.

He went on to add that he abhorred the 'tabloid journalism' of the Gazette that had in recent months fallen from its once impeachable fairness of reporting. He concluded his denouncement of the newspaper's claim by stating that whilst he naturally knew of the company Cobra Supplies he had only a passing acquaintanceship with its owners who he believed were upstanding businessmen and had, through their involvement in the Council's catering operations, brought a much needed improvement and commercial acumen.

Passing acquaintance thought Sid, well it seemed a lot chummier than that the other night at the council meeting. 'Anyway puss' remarked Sid as he felt the cat rubbing against his leg. 'I suppose you need feeding. Sorry I forgot this morning in my haste to get to the paper shop.'

As he forked out the meaty chunks into Fluffs 'dog bowl' he felt pleased that he had had a part in helping to expose some potential wrong doing at the council and wondered how the situation would evolve.

He didn't have long to wait as that night the situation at Creekleigh Council was headline news on the local television news programme.

Sid was a regular watcher of 'Towards the West' that preceded the main national news and was fascinated to see that evening's broadcast open with the familiar picture of the front of Creekleigh Council offices.

The news reporter explained that during the day, since the exposure that morning by the local paper, there had been considerable activity at the council offices. (Makes a change thought Sid. Whenever I have been there seems very little activity except for a huddle of two or three standing outside the main door having a fag.)

The reporter, who was standing on the steps of the offices, said that senior officers had been interviewed by police and papers had been taken away for examination. Councillor Hollingsworth, it was announced, had, as leader of the council, been invited to give an interview but had declined. Instead a statement had been issued on behalf of the council that confirmed that it was cooperating fully with the office of the Ombudsman and the police and that they had no further comments to add at this stage.

Ho, ho, thought Sid. This is becoming interesting, and so it did.

Within the next few days the local radio station advised that Councillor Bill Hollingsworth had been arrested in connection with misuse of his position as a councillor. It was claimed that he had, on a number of occasions, attempted to secure personal gain and that in relation to this a number of contracts entered into by the council were being investigated along with some planning decisions.

So by the time Tuesday came around and the date for Sid's lunch with Elizabeth, the problems surrounding Creekleigh District Council were deepening.

Chapter 26

As Sid walked into the Cozy Café he felt a tingle of excitement. Normally he only visited the place for a cup of coffee and chat with his old mate Cooper. But today he was having lunch with a lady and from whom he hoped to learn a bit more about the council and how she had been able to get the evidence to create the hiatus that currently existed at the town hall.

As Sid made his way through the tables and chairs set out in the small café he was quickly able to see that Elizabeth was already sitting at a table, with a reserved sign on it, towards which she beckoned him. As he approached she stood up and outstretched her hand and shook Sid's warmly.

The pair sat down with Sid, like an expectant child, unable to wait to hear from Elizabeth what the latest situation was.

'First things first Sid, lets order our meal then we can talk about whatever you wish.'

'Okay, I'll have the steak and kidney pud.'

'Would you like a starter Sid?'

'Oh well I don't usually but if you insist' he replied, scanning the top of the menu. 'I think I will have soup of the day.'

'Don't you want to know what it is before you order it?'

'No, not really, it's always mixed vegetable.'

Elizabeth smiled.

'Well, what about something to drink while you are waiting for your meal?'

Again Sid scanned the menu and decided to have a glass of old fashioned lemonade.

'Fine' responded his hostess who confirmed to the hovering waitress that she too would have the soup followed by a ham salad and a Perrier to drink.

The waitress duly nodded and headed off in the direction of the kitchen.

Elizabeth turned to Sid and began to explain to him in a low voice how she had been able, through her contacts, to tie the business operations of Cobra Supplies to some of those connected with the council and in particular the catering contract. From there, through a "mole" she had in the Council, she had been able to see how it was that vital decisions on the letting of contracts had been made outside of committees and without the correct scrutiny of either the councillors or their own finance department officers.

'Do you mean' inquired Sid, 'That Big Bill was fiddling the books.'

'No, not precisely Sid, what he was doing was making sure that whenever he wanted a specific organisation or individual to get a contract he was aware of who else was in the bidding process and the amount they were offering.'

'Oh I see, but what did he get out of it?'

'That's what the police are looking into now but I believe we will find that he was being paid handsomely by Mr Patel and that they also had joint business ventures and that through the planning system and Bill's position on the planning committee they were both able to profit from it. In fact Sid I have just found out this morning that Bill Hollingsworth's building construction company was likely to be involved in the demolition work of the Cobblers and his brother was to be the main contractor for the new restaurant.'

'How do you know this?' asked Sid in an uncharacteristic whisper.

'Well, apparently, the offices of Cobra Supplies were the subject of a police raid over the weekend and a number of papers were taken away. As a result of this I have been reliably informed that the planning decision on the Cobblers may have to be revoked and that this may not be the only one.'

'Does that mean,' asked Sid, 'that old Jacobson ain't got permission after all?'

'That's a strong possibility Sid but, as you know, both the police and the local government ombudsman are looking into the goings on and it will be for them to decided on individual cases if there has been maladministration and how it is to be remedied.'

'Great,' announced Sid forgetting for a moment his situation and suddenly realising that all the people in the café were staring at him.

Elizabeth smiled.

'Here comes our meal Sid I suggest you eat yours while it's hot and we can talk again later.'

Sid, consumed the last piece of potato on his plate, dragged the back of his hand across his lips and announced that the food had been good.

'What about a pudding' asked Elizabeth who by this time was aware that her lunch date liked his food.

She passed over a menu from a vacant adjacent table, which Sid briefly studied.

'It's got to be Spotted Dick and custard' replied Sid. 'My late wife use to make a lovely steamed pudding with really thick Birds Custard.'

With the pudding ordered the conversation continued.

'What happens next?' asked Sid.

'Well I suppose we now let the law take its course. The Ombudsman is likely to take weeks and weeks investigating the operations and decisions of the council and as for the police, well I think that the more they dig the more they will find. I doubt if Bill Hollingsworth will ever return to public duties and I understand that he will resign from the leadership at the next party meeting and probably from the council altogether as the pressure from the party will be too great for him to hang on. That's always assuming he is given bail and could in theory carry on.'

There was glint of glee in Sid's eyes as he then enquired about Mr Patel.

'Well' explained Elizabeth, 'I am not sure what is likely to become of Mr Patel. I think he is a very clever man but clearly he is likely to loose some or all of his contracts with the local authority and I am sure his operations will now also fall under the spotlight due to his obvious connections with Bill.'

'That was splendid' remarked Sid as his spoon scraped the last vestiges of custard from the side of the bowl.

'A cup of coffee to finish with' enquired his hostess.

'Thank ya, that would be lovely.'

The couple drank their coffees in relative silence as Sid thought over what had been discussed over the last hour or so and for her part Elizabeth became preoccupied with her thoughts on the enormity of what she had achieved and the shockwaves that her revelations had created through local politics.

Eventually Elizabeth rose from the table and went across to the counter of the café and paid the bill.

For his part Sid followed her from the tranquillity of the café into the busy High Street of Creekleigh.

Elizabeth again stretched out her hand to Sid and then in an act of impulse gave him a peck on the cheek and whispered, 'thank you Sid.'

The recipient was surprised by this unexpected action.

'You don't need to thank me I am just pleased that I might have had a small part to play in seeing the guilty get what they deserve.'

Elizabeth smiled. 'Bye Sid, keep in contact, you know where I work.'

At that she turned and walked away towards the Gazette offices leaving Sid staring after her and feeling very pleased with himself and life in general.

Sid walked back slowly along the High Street, mainly

because he had eaten so much that he could not hurry but also because he was so engrossed in his thoughts that the speed he was going was dictated by the lack of attention he was able to give to his surroundings.

As he approached his road (The Avenue) he rounded the corner and immediately noted that the sign over the Cobblers, which earlier in the week proclaimed 'SOLD', now read 'FOR SALE'.

'Allo, thought Sid, looks like Elizabeth's comments the other night on the phone that old Jacobson may not be retiring quite yet were spot on.

Sid stopped outside the shop and stared into the gloom of the interior through the traffic film stained window. He could see the cobbler working away at his last, but just as he was about to turn and walk away Jacobson raised his head and saw Sid's old knarled face staring in at him.

He gestured at Sid to enter and so it was with some degree of caution that he did as he was bid.

'I suppose your happy now Sid?'

'What do you mean happy?'

'Well as you can see from the sign outside the shop its up for sale again.'

'Why?'

'You ask why, haven't you been reading your local paper or watching the news. This bloody council of ours have been on some sodding fiddle and as a result Patel has dropped out of the sale and now they are saying that there was some malpractice in granting me planning permission and so not only have I lost a sale but probably any permission to change this place into anything else other than another shop.'

'Oh' exclaimed Sid.

'Well you might say oh Sid, that's my early retirement gone west. I don't expect any sympathy from you as I know you were dead against my selling up.'

'Now that's not true' responded Sid. 'What I was against was an Indian Restaurant on the site and all the implications it had for the people surrounding this place.'

'Well, alright, but this episode has left a bitter taste Sid do you understand what I mean.'

'Corse I do, we have known each other for donkey's years and I didn't want to end any friendship in the way we appeared to have done. I understand you were trying to make the best you could out of your shop sale and you must understand what I was trying to do.'

'Well yeah I suppose so, I just felt that on seeing you looking in through the window just then that maybe I had been a bit selfish.'

The two men stood facing each other for a moment and both felt tears welling up in their eyes. As if of one accord they simultaneously stretched out their right hand and each clasped the others tightly and smiled.

'See you around Sid.'

'Aye and you.'

Sid walked slowly out of the shop and along the road towards home happy in the knowledge that he had rekindled his friendship and that the Indian Restaurant proposal was no more. What was it, he thought to himself, that old Jacobson had said about his proposals. 'It's not what you know it's who you know.'

Sid smiled and walked through his litter-strewn front garden into his bungalow feeling rather pleased with life and still rather full!